AMBUSHED!

Morgan reached for his pistol and twisted in the saddle, sweeping the land with a searching gaze. An orange flower blossomed on a hill two hundred yards to the right. The crack of the bullet racketed Morgan's ears a split second after the air sizzled inches from his head.

He fired two futile shots and, swearing, rammed the pistol back in its leather and snatched the butt of the Winchester.

Another shot cracked in the stillness.

Morgan felt a hammering blow slam into his hip and he fought to keep from falling. Then as he brought the Winchester up to his shoulder another shot rang out.

The bullet caught Morgan low in the back, and suddenly he was pitching forward over the saddle horn . . .

TOMBSTONE SHOWDOWN

WALT DENVER

ZEBRA BOOKS

KENSINGTON PUBLISHING CORP.

ZEBRA BOOKS

are published by

Kensington Publishing Corp.
475 Park Avenue South
New York, NY 10016

First printing: January, 1990

Printed in the United States of America

CHAPTER ONE

Little Tommy Morgan stooped over to pick up another pretty stone for his growing collection. The sun struck the light from the quartz embedded in the pebble, blinding him for a moment. When he looked up, a shadow had fallen across him. The light from the stone disappeared. The sun was blotted out, gone.

Four men sat their horses, looking down at Tommy in his ragged pants and dusty shirt that was unbuttoned halfway down to his waist. He wore no shoes and the bottoms of his feet were caked with the same red dust that smeared his face.

He saw the men, and shivered slightly in the sudden chill from their shadows.

The men didn't smile at him.

They had whiskers on their faces. Their eyes were dark holes, shadowed, too, so that they appeared only as hollow sockets in hard faces. Their clothes were worn, dusty and they smelled of sour sweat and reeked of whiskey.

"Is that his kid?" asked Luke Trask, the leader. He

was a swarthy man with a bushy black mustache. He chewed on a matchstick stuck between his teeth. The end of the sulphur match was frayed, sodden with saliva. Pistols hung from his saddle horn, the same as the other men. Rifles jutted out of leather boots. All wore six-guns, tied low, in easy reach. They sat rugged, fine horses with good chests, strong limbs; dusty horses with alkali-caked nostrils and dust-rimmed eyes.

"About the right age," affirmed Fred Parsons, Trask's *segundo*. Parsons was whip-thin, with a lean, pinched face and puckered lips that were perpetually drawn up by a knife scar that ran from below his nose to his jawline.

"Same black, slick hair," commented Dave Higgins, a nervous, fidgety youth with spittle at the corners of narrow tight lips. Shoulder-length blond hair jutted ragged from under his battered leather hat.

"Ask him his name," said Harley Matling, a porky, squat man with a full beard, tiny feral eyes.

"What's your name, kid?" Trask asked gruffly.

"Tommy," said the boy, who was just over four years old.

"You kin to Chad Morgan?"

The boy nodded. "He's my papa . . . I gotta get back. I found some silver." He held up the quartz-streaked rock as if to appease the man asking the questions.

Matling snorted. "Thet ain't silver," he sneered.

"Yes it is!" the boy said, starting to edge away, out from under the shadow.

"Get him!" Trask commanded, extending an arm, a pointing finger.

Tommy's face froze with panic. His blue eyes glinted with sudden fear. He threw the rock at Matling, who

6

was swinging out of his saddle, and ran. Matling's foot caught in the stirrup and he cursed.

Higgins laughed and dug Spanish-roweled spurs into his bay's flanks. "I'll get the little bastard!" he yelled.

Tommy ran fast, past the cottonwoods that sprouted next to the dry creek bed down the slope, screaming, "Mama!" Tears gushed from his eyes, streamed down his face. *"Tío Pedro! Mamá! Papá!"* His shrieks floated shrill on the dry Arizona air, echoed in the low redrock hills.

Higgins jerked a lariat free of the saddle ring, shook out a loop, taking his time, enjoying the game. He dropped the single strap rein over the saddle horn, began swinging his *riata*, widening the loop.

Tommy Morgan, sobbing, out of breath, topped a rise, saw the adobe house, and shrieked again. His mother burst from the cabin, moving as fast as she could, hampered by a long cotton dress and apron, and the *huaraches*—woven Mexican sandals—she wore in summer. Her long, braided hair, like spun gold, flopped in twin strands as she struggled to reach her son.

Pedro Gomez, whom the boy called uncle, but who in fact was not related to him, spit out the nail in his teeth, pushed aside the horse he was shoeing, and began to run after Bonnie Morgan. He, too, had heard the screams and now he saw the horseman chasing little Tommy with a whirling rope. Tío Pedro gripped the blacksmith's hammer tightly in his hand.

Higgins threw the loop. It sailed gracefully through the air and dropped over the tad's shoulders. When it encircled his waist, Higgins jerked the rope. His horse, trained to take up the slack, dug in its hooves and pulled the rope taut, quartering in the opposite direction. Tommy Morgan skidded on his rump, backward, and screamed in terror.

"My God! Stop it! Leave Tommy alone!" Bonnie's face contorted in rage, and stumbling, she got up, frantic.

The other three horsemen pounded up over the rise.

Tío Pedro chased after Higgins whose horse was still backing up. Tommy bounced along the hard earth, his wails blood-curdling cries of fright. Pedro brandished the hammer in his hand, cursed in Spanish.

Higgins clawed for his pistol.

Bonnie ran toward her son, tears flooding her face.

Harley Matling jerked his Winchester from its scabbard, levered a shell in the chamber. He reined his mount to a stop, took aim before Higgins could draw his six-gun. He shot Tío Pedro in the head, leading him a foot, squeezing the trigger. The Mexican's head exploded in a cloud-spray of pink blood. He skidded facedown into the dust, his legs twitching spasmodically.

Bonnie saw Tío Pedro go down. She screamed again.

Higgins drew his pistol, holstered it again quickly. Before the woman could reach her son, he rammed his spurs into the horse's flanks. The gelding bolted away, dragging the screaming boy after him. The boy turned over and over, bumped along the ground.

Trask and Matling rode up to the woman. Trask's horse reared. Bonnie tried to escape, go after her son, but Matling cut her off, laughing at the sport.

"Let me alone!" Bonnie rasped.

Higgins stopped dragging the boy.

Tommy was still, his face bruised and bloodied. A lump swelled on his forehead. His tiny legs didn't move.

Bonnie saw him, ran around Harley Matling's horse,

and shambled awkwardly to her son's side. She sobbed and began trying to pull the rope from his waist. His face was turning blue. The rope was so tight. She picked him up in her arms, began breathing into his mouth. The boy's chest heaved as he sucked in air. His eyelids fluttered open and closed. Bonnie held his frail body to hers and shook with heavy sobbing.

A hand on her arm jerked her roughly to her feet.

Fred Parsons stared at the hysterical woman. Her golden hair was streaked with red dust where she had fallen. Her face was scratched from the stones, her pale-blue eyes shone with a mixture of madness and fear. She was a beautiful woman, nonetheless. Her beauty was plain to see despite her anguished state. Full breasts tugged at the bodice of her cotton dress. Her ankles were slim, her hips curved, buttocks rounded.

The scar on Parsons's face flared white as he flushed a dark rose. Spittle formed at the corners of his mouth.

His whiskey breath blew fetid on Bonnie's face.

She cringed, shrank away from him.

Parsons tightened his grip on her arm. The blood drained away from her arm as his fingers slipped slightly, leaving gaunt marks in her flesh.

"Pretty little thang, ain't she?" Harley Matling grinned, riding up. Trask swung down from his horse, and Higgins started playing out the rope. He slid from his saddle, loosened it from the boy's waist, and coiled it back up as he walked away from Tommy, his eyes on the woman. Tommy lay still, his chest moving imperceptibly, color returning to his cheeks. A trickle of blood seeped from one corner of his mouth, but no one noticed.

"Gimme her!" Trask shoved Parsons aside, snatched both of Bonnie's pigtails up in his hand.

Parsons sidestepped away, glaring.

"D-don't hurt me," Bonnie pleaded. "Let me see my boy."

"Where's your man?" Trask demanded, twisting the braids cruelly.

Pain contorted Bonnie's face. Her eyes closed, opened again.

"I ast you a question, lady! Where's Chad Morgan?"

"He . . . he'll be back any minute," Bonnie lied craftily. "He'll kill you for this!"

Trask snorted and laughed. "He ain't anywheres near. Over to Fort Huachuca, I reckon."

"Harley," he said, "you and Fred check out the house. Higgins, you look around, see if anybody else is about."

Reluctantly, the men scattered and walked off unsteadily on uncertain boot heels. Higgins looked back once, to see what Trask was doing with the woman.

Trask released his grip on Bonnie's hair. She staggered backward a pace.

"Well, Chad done got himself set up right smart," he said. "Five years I been hunting that sneaky bastard. Looks like I finally found out where he holed up with his whore. Remember my brother, Ned Trask? You and Chad set up Ned and he's dead all these years."

"We didn't," Bonnie whimpered. "Luke Trask, Chad didn't do no wrong. Ned was at fault. Please, let me go to my boy. He's hurt."

"In time, little lady. First, you and me got some business."

There was no mistaking his leer. Bonnie Morgan drew back, shrank away from him, terrified. She put her hand to her mouth. Trask stared at the wedding ring on her finger. Sunlight sparkled in the depths of its tiny stones.

"All clear, Trask!" Parsons shouted.

"Same here!" Higgins echoed, stalking through the stables after checking the bunkhouse where Tío Pedro had lived.

Trask grabbed Bonnie's wrist and jerked her toward the house. She screamed, knowing it would do no good. No one could hear—no one who cared.

"What're you goin' to do, Luke?" Parsons asked.

"Put the boots to his whore, that's what."

"Haw! That'll learn him!" Parsons laughed.

"Seconds!" Harley Matling called out.

"Thirds!" Higgins rapped, running up from the stables.

"Shit," Parsons said.

Trask shoved Bonnie inside the house. It was a low adobe with a sod roof. Sparsely furnished, it was neat, with homemade furniture, flowers in a clay vase, a living room, kitchen, and dining area, one large bedroom, and a smaller one for Tommy. Trask found the bedroom he wanted and pushed Bonnie through the door. It was cool and dark inside.

"Don't, please," Bonnie begged. "Let me go."

Trask kicked the door shut, his boot heel slamming into the wood. The door swung to on leather hinges, rattled in the jamb. Then he lashed out at Bonnie, grabbed the bodice of her dress. There was a sickening gnash of ripping cloth. He stared at her bared breast

11

jutted out ripe as a melon from her chest. His eyes widened. His loins stirred with desire.

"Well, now," he whispered, "you're right purty, little lady. The years ain't done you no harm."

"God, please. Don't," she whimpered, cringing.

Trask grabbed her, forced heavy, wet lips on hers. She tightened up. He drew back, slapped her.

Tears welled in her eyes.

He grabbed her torn dress, ripped it completely off, then stared at the blond patch between her legs, shielded by thin panties.

Bonnie tried to cover her nakedness. She drew her hands up over her breasts, twisted her legs, pressed them close together.

Trask dropped his pants and gunbelt.

He forced her onto the bed, pried her legs apart. He straddled her, then plunged into her sheath.

Bonnie screamed in stark horror.

A darkness rose up in her mind, drowned her senses.

Mercifully, she passed out as Trask rammed deep, plundering the wife of the man he hated.

CHAPTER TWO

Morgan headed his horse east toward the Little Dragoons. He was glad he had decided against going to Tombstone with Curly Garth and the boys. He'd have lost two days there—at least another day in travel. Hell, it had been tempting. They had gotten a good price for the herd at Fort Huachuca and after he'd paid off the boys, he still had plenty left. A saddlebag full of pretties for Bonnie and Tommy, a new fry pan, an *olla* hanging from the saddle horn so that they could have *tepache* and sip it in the heat of the day or in the cool of the Arizona evening. Bonnie would be pleased. She was a good woman and she had borne him a strong son.

Chad Morgan worried the hunk of Climax chewing tobacco in his mouth. Around the house he didn't indulge in such luxury, but on the drive, or working cattle, it kept a man's thirst in check, took down the nerves a notch when ragging after a mossy horn or taming a contrary mustang. He was a tall, lean man with a shock of raven-dark hair under his Stetson, deep-blue eyes, a cleft chin, wide strong shoulders.

"Pick it up, Captain Joe," he said to his horse. Benson was a long stretch behind him and he could see the Dragoons against the sky. His shadow was pulling out ahead of him, getting longer as the sun dipped toward the western horizon.

Captain Joe was a coal-black gelding, sixteen hands high with four white stockings. He moved under a California saddle, and the blood of Arabian and Morgan breeds ran in his veins. Besides being a beauty, he was a working cow-horse, Morgan's favorite among his *remuda*. He could cover forty mile a day and never show it. With his good lungs and good legs, he was a solid mount, the quickest bar none Morgan had ever ridden or roped from.

The gelding responded to the gentle nudge of single-bit spurs touched to his flanks. He broke into an easy canter and Morgan started whistling a tuneless ditty. The spring air was crisp and there would be frost in the high country come morning.

Morgan stopped whistling when he saw them. Buzzards—circling high in the sky over his ranch.

The air took on a deeper chill, and he flipped up the collar of his light buckskin jacket.

There were a lot of buzzards. From a distance, with eyes squinted, they almost looked like a column of smoke. But there was no smoke, only circling turkey buzzards wheeling in vertical patterns.

Morgan kicked Captain Joe into a gallop, the *olla* bouncing so hard he had to hold it to keep it from breaking or injuring his horse.

He stopped short on the hill overlooking his ranch buildings.

It was quiet.

Something was wrong.

Dead wrong.

Two buzzards were on the ground, strutting around a large object. A cow. Or a man. A horse stood underneath the shed, where Tío Pedro did his shoeing. He was haltered, and there was no smoke rising from the brazier.

Morgan scanned the ranch compound. There was not a sign of life.

He reached into his shirt pocket and pulled out two wads of cotton and put one in each ear. Then he drew his pistol, a Remington .44. He hammered back, aimed it at the ground. Fired one shot. Smoke and flame belched from the long barrel of the .44. Dirt kicked up a few yards away. Captain Joe held steady.

The two buzzards on the ground flapped into the air, lifted lazily into the sky. The flying buzzards flared away from the sound, scattered like leaves blown before a wind.

But no one came outside to look. Not Bonnie. Not Tommy. Not Tío Pedro.

Morgan holstered the .44. He did not remove the cotton from his ears. A sickness began to build in his stomach. The muscles in his jaws quivered, knotted.

Captain Joe moved out as Morgan clucked to him, raked his flanks gently with the knobby spurs. Morgan's eyes flickered as they moved in their sockets, scanning the rolling hills, the outcroppings of red rocks. The sun was low on the horizon now, the shadows of the horse and man long on the reddish earth. The chill in the air deepened. There was no breeze. It was as if the silence itself was a muffled shriek in his ears. He took out the wads of cotton, but it was no different.

There was a stench in the air. The queasiness in his stomach boiled up again and he tasted the faint acid of bile in his throat.

He rode over to Pedro Gomez's body first, to confirm his gut feeling.

"Christ," he muttered.

The back of Tío Pedro's head was blown away. A round blue-black hole gaped in the center of his forehead. Flies and ants fought over the dried blood. The buzzards had taken out his eyes.

Morgan leaned out to the side and vomited, the bile rising up in his throat with a gagging rush. He retched until his eyes watered and his stomach grew claws. Captain Joe shied from the vomit, sidestepping away from the stench. Morgan held on to the saddle horn, weak, helpless, then he straightened up, the sickness replaced by a steel ball in the pit of his stomach.

The ball turned ice-cold, freezing his innards.

Morgan knew what it was: fear.

He slid out of the saddle. Stood on wobbly legs. His knees were jelly.

"Bonnie!" he screamed. "Bonnie, for God's sake!"

Then he started running toward the house. Running on uneven boot heels. Running through thick mud that slowed him down when he wanted to fly. Running through airless space into a void that he could feel like a thickening in his throat.

The front door was open.

Morgan raced through, afraid of what he would find. "Bonnie?"

The front room was empty. There was no answer. Morgan stopped short, listened to the awful ticking of silence.

Then a low whimper came from the back bedroom.

"Bonnie?" He stalked through the doorway, down the hall. The door to their bedroom was open. He went inside, saw her in the gloom. Saw her form, felt her presence, heard her moan. He ran to the bedside, looked down. She was holding something in her arms.

"Tommy!"

She was naked, shivering. Her eyes were closed. He drew open the curtains. The sunset was a raw wound in the sky. There was enough light for him to see her better, see his son staring up at him with wide, fearful eyes. Tenderly, he lifted his son in his arms. He felt light, too light, as if something had gone out of him.

"No! Don't!" Tommy screamed when his father touched him.

"Tommy, it's me. Papa. Don't you know me, boy?"

"Papa! Some mens hurt me. I'm scared."

His father looked at him closely—his haunted eyes and quivering mouth, blood, dried and caked, at the corners. Tommy winced when Morgan moved him slightly. He lifted his son's dirty shirt, saw the hideous marks on the boy's flesh. It was then that he heard the soft wheezing when the boy breathed. He touched the lad's ribs gingerly.

Tommy screamed in pain.

"I'm sorry," said his father. "Did they hit you?"

The boy shook his head, and even that slight movement caused him pain.

Chad Morgan laid the boy down on the bed. He was gentle, but even so, little Tommy cringed and whimpered.

"I want to see how your mother is," he told the boy.

"Mama's hurt. She's asleep."

Morgan's lips tightened as he turned Bonnie over, looked at her in the fading light. Her eyes were puffed, swollen with purple bruises. Her lips were smashed to a bloody pulp and an egg-size lump distorted her cheekbone on one side of her face. There were purplish smudges on her neck.

Then he looked at her loins.

Bloody smears covered her inner thighs. Massive bruises on her flesh, yellow and purple. He saw the dried blood on the bedclothes then.

Her breasts.

The ugliest sight of all. Cigarette burns. More bruises. A nipple bit half in two, encrusted with dried blood.

Morgan sat beside his wife, touched her face.

"Bonnie. It's me, Chad. Bonnie?"

Her eyes fluttered. Opened. A moan rattled her throat. She winced in pain.

"Chad? Is it really you?"

"What happened here?"

"I . . . I thought I was dead . . . Tommy?"

"He's here. Hurt bad. What did they do to him? He looks like a horse stepped on him."

"Rope. They roped him. Dragged him . . ."

"Who, Bonnie? Dammit, who?" He fought to control his anger, struggled to quell the rage storming inside him. But he had to know, had to know who had done these terrible things to his wife and son. He had to know everything.

"Trask," she said, her voice a trembling whisper, a painful effort at speech.

"Trask?"

A shadow passed over Morgan's face. He had not

heard that name in a long time. Ned Trask had courted Bonnie, too, when she was Bonnie Lewis, back in Ellsworth, Kansas Territory. They had both been in love with Bonnie. But Ned was one of a wild bunch who were sons of men who had turned outlaw after the War Between the States, men who inherited from their fathers and older brothers the lust for preying on helpless people.

Ned Trask. Memories of another time. Ned was Morgan's principal rival for the hand of Bonnie Lewis in marriage. He had been content to let Bonnie make up her own mind. Trask had, too, in the beginning. When she made her choice, it was different. Bonnie had picked him, Chad Morgan. Ned had taken it hard, so hard he had called Morgan out. Crazy. It was supposed to be a fair fight, but it wasn't. Ned had two friends in on it. His older brother was out of town that day. Luke Trask. It was too bad he hadn't been there. The fight was rigged. Ned and two homeless drifters named Akers and Worman braced Morgan down at the cattle pens.

Chad had taken all three men out that day. And no one had seen him do it, except Bonnie. She had been terrified.

There was so much shooting, Chad's ears had rung for a long time afterward. It was chase and shoot through the pens. A child's game with real bullets. And Chad Morgan had killed three men.

He was just twenty years old.

Luke Trask claimed that Chad had started the fight. He had a loud mouth and he said it so often that people believed him. Bonnie was shunned as the woman who had caused it all, the woman who was responsible for the taking of three young lives. No one had given a damn about Akers and Worman before that, but they ended up as poor lost boys who had been murdered along with Ned Trask.

Chad and Bonnie had to go into hiding.

They put a price on Chad Morgan's head.

He had to flee from the law in Ellsworth—and from Luke Trask. He lived under the constant shadow of the gun.

Bonnie and Chad were married in Fort Hays. They moved to Dodge City, where Tommy was born. Then they had to move again and again, from place to place as his past caught up with him.

Finally, driven out of the Kansas Territory, Morgan headed southwest, taking cattle from the borderlands of Texas and Mexico—strays in the *barrancas*—building his herd, getting a stake in country where faceless men with no names or false men lived lawless lives. Morgan never changed his name, as so many others had, because he knew he wasn't guilty of murder as they said he was.

Now, after five years of running, Luke Trask had caught up with him.

"Bonnie," he said softly, leaning over her, "did he . . . did Trask . . ."

Bonnie nodded bitterly. "He . . . he raped me, Chad. Then, the others."

"Who are they? What are their names?"

Her eyes widened. He saw the fury smoldering in their depths. He saw the pain of remembering in the smoke of her anger, the swirling light of hatred dancing in the pale-blue seas. It was like looking into hell and up to a righteous heaven all at once. It was like looking

20

at a woman being tortured, driven to the brink of madness, then brought to life again only to suffer a nameless horror, a horror that was as endless as eternity. As hellfire. As the sleep of death itself.

"Harley Matling, Fred Parsons, and the worst of all, Dave Higgins." She said their names clearly, the vowels solid, the consonants crisp. "I'll never forget them. I'll never forget their ugly, cruel faces. Luke Trask knew you were gone. Knew where you were. He planned this. Higgins roped little Tommy. He roped him and dragged him, and Luke Trask wouldn't let me go to him. They raped me, Chad, and they broke something inside our son. They broke me. I'm dying . . ."

"No!" he rasped. "No!"

She reached out her hand, touched his lips. "Don't say anything. There isn't much time. I heard their names. I've been saying them over and over. Damning them! Hating them! Cursing them! Kill them, Chad. Kill every one of them. Kill them for me. And for Tommy!"

There was a rattle in her throat. A gasp escaped her lips. Chad lunged for her, grabbed her shoulders, shook her as tears burst from his eyes. He pleaded with her, prayed for her, begged her.

But she was gone.

Bonnie was gone forever.

CHAPTER THREE

The campfire bounced flickers of orange light on the steep walls of the canyon. Shadows danced like macabre demons under the overhang of the ledge. The bottle, passed from hand to hand, swarmed with an amber light. The moon bathed the talus slopes with a pewter haze, furred the rimrock with dull silver. Stars sprinkled the blue-black sky, winking, sputtering, glaring, appearing close enough to reach out and touch, but, in reality, far enough away to be in a past that no man had ever seen.

Harley Matling wiped his beard, grunted from the bowels of his swollen belly. He stared at Luke Trask with small bead-bright eyes that wandered in and out of focus.

"That was some chunk," he slobbered. "Don't know why in hell we didn't stay for another run at the trough."

"Yeah," Dave Higgins said, lying away from the fire, his boots stacked atop a flat stone. "That was prime meat, Trask."

"I reckon Luke had his reasons," Parsons said, reasserting his status as *segundo*. "Woman was done in. Like stokin' a dead fire—poker moves, but the ashes is plumb cold."

Trask swilled deep from the bottle. Passed it to Parsons. His shadow moved under the overhang. The temperature had dropped sharply after sundown. The men had on their sheepskin coats. Whiskey in their bellies mixed with the hardtack and bacon-drenched beans. He swayed on his perch, a round cousin to a boulder that had rolled from its height on some long-ago midnight. He scratched numb fingers across the bristle that lined his face. Another hand produced a matchstick, its end frayed and wet, which he screwed into the corner of his mouth.

"I had reasons," Trask said, his tongue thick from drink. "You heard what she said? Her bastard husband due in any time. I want the sombitch to know. I want Chad Morgan to know it was me what sulled his woman. The woman that should have been my brother's wife. The bitch! The whore!"

"I thought they was a time when you wanted to kill that jasper Morgan," Harley said. "On sight. And we make that long trip up here and you don't do nothin' but work over his slut."

Trask belched, worked the match around in his mouth. "You got it right, Harley. After he killed my brother, I wanted to blow his fuckin' head off. I wanted to jerk his nuts out by the roots and stuff 'em in his mouth. I carried that grudge a powerful long time. And then I met a man who changed my mind. Smart man."

Higgins sat up, interested. He was not as drunk as the others. Mellow, sated with food and drink, still tingling from the afternoon at the Morgan rancho. Thinking of that woman's creamy thighs, the way she screamed when he shoved up inside her. "Who was that?" Higgins asked.

Trask tweaked his black mustache. He had never told the story before. Maybe now was the time. See how it rode on these men, his friends. "Feller's name was Neeli Larimer. An old mountain man I met up with in Wyoming, over to Fort Laramie. Neeli had a lot of savvy. I heard tell of a man up that way that could have been Chad Morgan. Fast with a gun, had a wife, kinda quiet. Ran into Neeli Larimer at a dry camp with plenty of whiskey. Asked about Morgan. It was him all right, but he had done rode on time I got there. I got some likkered up, told Neeli Larimer what I aimed to do with Morgan when I caught up to him. Well, he just reared back his shaggy old head and laughed fit to bust."

"How come?" Higgins asked, leaning forward, his face shimmering in the firelight.

"Neeli Larimer ups and asks me did I suffer much after Brother Ned died. I tell him shore and that I had put a lot of pride in that kid and wanted him to grow up and all. So, Neeli, he asks me how it felt to hurt all that time and know that little Ned would never grow no more and never be a full-growed man. Well, I don't get his drift, but I allow as how I felt robbed by this Morgan bastard and I aimed to kill him same as he killed Ned."

"Well, what in hell's wrong with that?" Harley blurted.

"Yair, that's what I woulda done," Parsons said cautiously. "I reckon. An eye for an eye."

Trask cocked one eye and looked at the two men as if they had lost their senses. He moved the matchstick to the front of his mouth, spewed it out into the fire. It hissed briefly and burst into flame. "Same as I told Neeli Larimer back then—two, three years ago, afore I met you fellers. He put me straight, all right. Said the worst thing I could do was to kill Morgan. Put him out of his misery. Yessir, he was some smart man, old Neeli. He said that the onliest way to get even with Chad Morgan was to make him suffer like I done. I mean downright hard-ass suffer. He said he learned that from books he read once't. Greek stories, I think. All about sufferin' and guilt and stuff."

"That don't make any sense at all," Higgins said, a note of wonder in his voice.

"Oh, it does, boy, it does," Trask said, warming to his audience. "Said if you hated a man, really hated him all through your bones, you didn't kill him. That was easy. And it was all over. Dead is out of pain, out of trouble. I saw some sense in that, but I said I'd rest better knowin' Morgan was where my brother was, wherever that was—heaven, hell, or six feet under with the worms. And Larimer asked how I'd feel if Ned hadn't been killed but had just had his arms and legs tore off. Or how I'd feel if somebody put out both my eyes or cut off my privates. I said it would be pure hell, living the life of a damned cripple."

"Yeah," Higgins breathed.

"I don't see the point," Harley said impatiently.

"Well, now, Neeli Larimer explained that the whole bone of contention 'twixt my brother and Morgan was that gal, Bonnie. Said as how he'd seen the two and they were some stuck on one another. Said if I could

25

not find this Morgan and cut off something real important like his feet or his hands, then the best thing would be to do something to his woman and his kid. Make the bastard suffer like I suffered. Not for just a few minutes, but all the rest of his born days. And that's what we done, shore enough. I'd give a poke of gold to see Morgan's face when he sees his woman all torn up, her hole all ripped and brimful of my seed. And, Higgins, you did a fair job on that kid. He's got at least a coupla busted ribs and his guts are mush. He won't live out the week."

Dave Higgins whistled in frank admiration. "You are some *hombre*," he said. "I thought we was just havin' fun."

"We was," Trask said, gesturing for the bottle. Parsons handed it to him. "Thing is, we ain't done yet. Harley, you and Fred mosey on back there tomorry and see if Morgan's come back yet. Don't show yourselfs if'n you can he'p it, and meet me and Dave in Tombstone soon as you find out what Morgan does. Maybe his whore will die. If she does, he'll bury her. And the kid won't make it."

"What if he sees us?" Harley asked.

"I'd be purely disappointed," Trask said, taking a healthy swig from the whiskey bottle. "I reckon that would make me real mad."

"Morgan has any guts, he'll come after you, Luke," Parsons said. "From what you told us, he don't back down much."

"He's been runnin' from me for five years, ain't he? Neeli Larimer said Morgan was right smart with pistol and knife, but he's harder to track than a mountain goat. I think when he sees his wife like that, he'll just

26

suck air. Thing is, I want to know. I want to know that bastard's sufferin'."

The bottle went around again. Dave Higgins took a bigger pull this time. He looked at Trask with new-found respect. He wanted Trask to respect him. He was the newest of the bunch and didn't have the experience of the others. Luke Trask was well known along the owlhoot trail. It was a lucky day for him when he met Trask. They had lived well, without working too hard or getting the law on them. They'd rustled a few cattle here and there, rolled drunks, held up a stage when it wasn't too dangerous, ran a few horses off ranches and sold them to buyers who didn't care much about brands or bills of sale. It was a good life, with hardly any responsibility. They always had plenty of money and Trask generally had a pretty good idea where the next dollar was coming from. This had been a side trip. A favor to Trask. He just wished he had known about Neeli Larimer before they had put the boots to Morgan's woman.

"We'll ride back to Morgan's in the mornin'," Fred told Trask. "Early. Harley, you better hold back on the tanglefoot, else you'll ride with a head too big for your sombrero."

"Yair," Harley drawled. "We get to Tombstone we can rustle up some whiskey that doesn't burn your ass-hole for a week afterward."

Trask stood up, stretched. His shadow loomed large on the rock wall. Higgins threw another stick on the fire. He was wide awake, didn't want the talk to stop.

"How come you don't go back yourself to see how this Morgan feller takes up the slack on the rope you left him?" Higgins asked.

Trask sat down, started pulling on his boot heel. Fred and Harley laid out their bedrolls up against the wall that reflected the heat from the fire. They seemed disinterested in hearing any more talk. Morning was not so far off that they wanted to linger.

"Dave, you got a head on your shoulders, but you don't think too swift sometimes. Morgan knows my face. He don't know Fred or Harley from Adam. And was I you I wouldn't be too keen on Morgan knowing who you was, either."

"You afraid of him?"

"Shit! Afraid?"

"Was your brother fast? With a gun?"

Trask grunted as the boot came off. His sock was grimy, sodden with sweat. He tugged it off, laid it on a rock to dry. Its smell was gamy. He got a grip on the other boot. "Ned was some fast. Practiced all the time. But shootin' a man ain't easy. Any big animal can spook you. I 'member my first turkey. Big bird. In the woods, over the sights of a Greener, the critter looked bigger'n a barn. I shook some. Then, you go after your first deer. Even bigger. And I shook like a dog shittin' peach seeds. But a man, that's the worst. I guess Ned didn't have the stomach to kill Morgan by hisself. He had help, and Morgan got them, too."

"Maybe Morgan had help."

Trask shook his head. "Nope. He did it by hisself. Three men shot square in the front. And each of them had burnt powder. Their barrels proved that. Smelled. So they got their turns."

"Sounds to me like you got some respect for this Morgan."

Trask cursed the air blue and wrenched the other

boot from his foot. His sock came part ways off with it. He flung it on the rock, glared at Higgins. "I don't respect him. He still killed my brother. I think he done it dirty, but I can't prove it. Suckered him some way. You know, like pretending to give up and then shooting him. Ned might not have had much guts, but he was fast. And he was careful. That's why he got hisself help. Wrong help, though."

Trask rubbed his dirty feet—between the toes, on top of the arch. Parsons and Matling crawled into their bedrolls fully clothed. They didn't say good night and were both snoring in seconds.

Higgins got his bedroll, walked back to the fire. He stared into it a long time. Trask watched him, then yawned. The kid was thinking mighty hard. He had something in his craw. It would come out. Now or sometime. He was a good kid. Would be with seasoning. He had nerve and that counted for something. He was fast, too. Reminded him a lot of Ned. Hell, he still missed his kid brother. Maybe Higgins was somehow taking his place.

"Luke," Higgins said after a while. "What do you think this Morgan will do? Will he come after us?"

Trask frowned. He picked up a stick, roiled the fire, tossed it in. Stepping away from the fire, his face disappeared in shadow, the dark points of his mustache jutting out from his silhouette. He took off his hat, wiped the sweatband. "He might. Hard tellin' what grief will do to a man. We hurt him, kid, hurt him bad. Man's got iron in his backbone, he'll rear up and go after what hurt him."

"I'm not afraid of him."

"Nope? You ain't never met him."

"Last time you saw him he was just a kid like me, wasn't he? He impress you much?"

"Back then? I didn't like him none because he was sparkin' Ned's gal. He was on the quiet side. Hard to figger someone like that. I'd say he'll likely buck with a burr under his saddle, that one. You likely don't want to run into him. Neeli Larimer had some things to say about him."

"Oh? Like?"

"Like a man called him out at the Cheyenne Saloon. A gunny. Morgan didn't back down."

"He killed him?"

"Worse. He whupped him, run him out of town. Could've killed him, though. But he run the jasper out, tail tucked 'twixt his legs."

"That don't sound like much."

"Way Neeli Larimer told it, did. Anyways, the jasper come back spoilin' fer a fight. Morgan accommodated him."

"Huh?"

"Yep. Killed him clean the second time. Larimer said nobody bothered Morgan much after that. And I guess that might make some men think a time er two 'fore tanglin' with him."

Higgins gave a low whistle. "You think I could beat him, Luke?"

Trask shook his head. He dug out something from his vest pocket, held it up to the firelight. The tiny diamonds scintillated with light.

"Not till you're tempered some. Morgan's been over the trail. 'Sides, he's got more reason to kill you than you have him. Better make sure he never finds out you were out there today."

Higgins looked hurt. His face hardened, then went slack. Trask smiled in the shadows. He put the ring back in his vest pocket, unrolled his blankets, kicked them into position some distance from the fire.

After the two men were in their bedrolls, Higgins thought of something else to say.

"Luke. You still awake?"

"Yair."

"Meant to ask you. How come you knew that Morgan wouldn't be there today?"

Trask laughed quietly. "I was wonderin' when someone'd ask, kid. Reason I got to go to Tombstone. To pay off a man what told me that little secret. Yessir, he done me a big favor. And it's gonna cost me only thirty dollars."

"Who?"

"A man named Curly. Curly Garth. He's Morgan's *segundo*. And I knowed Curly a long, long time."

The fire crackled. Sparks flew up in the air. Dave Higgins stared at it for several moments. Then he closed his eyes and thought about a man named Morgan.

CHAPTER FOUR

Tommy looked up at his father with wide, pain-filled eyes. "It hurts," he said.

"I know, Son. I have to see if those ribs'll set. This is a tight wrapping."

"I can't breathe."

"It's gonna be hard for a while."

Chad Morgan finished wrapping the torn sheet around Tommy's ribs. He allowed room for him to breathe, tied the knot tight. He wished that was all there was to it. Tommy's ribs weren't the worst part of it, he knew. Something was broken inside the boy. Something serious. He didn't know enough about a person's innards to know how bad it was, but he guessed the spleen might be damaged, a kidney maybe. The boy winced every time he touched any spot on his frail body.

"Where's Mama?"

"She's asleep, Tommy."

"I wanta sleep with her."

"You can't, Tommy. That's how come I brought a

bunk in here. I'm gonna sleep right close to you." He had given the boy powders, but the fever was rising every minute. He didn't like little Tommy's color, either. His chest and ribs were blue-black-yellow, but his face was pale as chalk. He didn't have the heart to tell him his mother was dead. He had washed her up, put on her prettiest flannel nightgown. Touched some rouge to her cheeks and combed her hair. She lay on her bed now, her eyes closed, her hands folded across her tummy. He couldn't bear to look at her, yet he had held her hand for a long time before he realized it was cold and hard and lifeless.

He laid the boy in his bed, felt his forehead. Hot. Sweaty. He tucked a toy animal in Tommy's arms. The boy ignored his favorite sleeping companion, a squirrel he called Rusty.

"I'm cold, Papa."

Morgan drew the blankets up over the boy. Tommy hadn't eaten. The water he'd taken had come right back up, laced with blood. The boy had turned blue, choked on his own vomit. It had been touch and go for a while. That was hours ago.

Yet Chad wasn't tired. Something was burning deep inside him and he didn't know what it was. He was faced with a death he couldn't understand. With a sick boy he couldn't help. That was the worst part. Looking into Tommy's eyes, seeing the hurt there and feeling so helpless that he had come close to anger several times. Wanted to shout at Tommy to straighten up, get well! But he had quelled the emotion, smothered it until it raged like a fever in his brain.

"Tommy, you sleep well. Hear."

"I want Mama."

He'd tell him tomorrow when he buried her. Tomorrow was soon enough. No use giving the boy nightmares. He would have them anyway. Chad couldn't forget how frightened Tommy had been when he had first seen him, his own father. He thought the man with the rope was coming back to get him. He was afraid of all men now. And Chad couldn't blame him.

Which one had done that? In questioning the boy he had tried not to guide his answers. Tommy had done pretty well, though. A young man, with long, ragged blond hair had done the roping. Tommy had been sure about that. He described the others, but not as well. Just that they were older men, mean-looking men, terrible men. But he couldn't forget the younger one. Morgan wouldn't forget him, either.

He had four names, but the only one he could put a face to was Luke Trask. What about Fred Parsons, Harley Matling, and Dave Higgins? Which one was the roper? Where were they headed? Dragoon? Tucson? El Paso? Las Cruces? Or north, to Santa Fe? Or Taos, maybe. There were a thousand towns, a dozen directions.

But now was not the time to think of revenge. There was a burying to do and a hurt boy to nurse.

Chad stroked his son's forehead. His mother would often sing the lad to sleep, crooning him a lullaby that she'd often made up as she went along. Another memory. Bonnie had been a good mother, better than most. Tommy worshipped her. He would miss her something fierce. They both would.

The boy ought to see a doctor, but Chad knew it would be risky to move him.

He would need someone to look after him, too. A woman. Someone to take the place of his mother.

Chad hung his head, burying it in the palms of his hands.

No one could take the place of Bonnie.

And what woman did he know within twenty miles?

That was the problem with staying off the beaten path. Of being alone. A man didn't have many neighbors. His friends were few and far between.

He looked at Tommy. The boy was asleep. Morgan stood up, turned down the lamp. He would leave it lighted for a while. If the boy woke up he wouldn't be so scared. He walked to the window, opened it so he could hear if Tommy cried out. He had two graves to dig and he didn't want to leave that chore until morning. Besides, he needed to do something, anything, to drain off the energy flowing through his muscles. He guessed it was a combination of grief and anger. But there was frustration there, too. Four men had ridden onto his place, killed his hired man, hurt his son, and violated his wife. Just like that.

As if they had known he was gone!

Morgan took another look at Tommy, then left the room. He stalked through the empty house, passing the door to his own bedroom. It was shut. He stopped, listened, as if to hear her breathing, as if to hear her call his name. Tears stung his eyes. He wiped them quickly with a finger and thumb and tiptoed past the room to the kitchen.

Lighting a lamp with a sulphur match, adjusting the wick, he found the Arbuckle's—the coffee pot. He fished through the coffee can for the cinnamon stick. It was at the bottom. For Tommy. Arbuckle's always put a cinnamon stick in with the beans to keep them fresh. Bonnie had always given Tommy the "surprise" and he was glad that it was still there. He poured beans in the grinder, turned the crank. The aroma of fresh-ground coffee was overpowering, made him miss Bonnie all the more. He put the coffee and water in the pot. It was the only way he knew to make coffee.

The night air was chill. Morgan rattled in the tack-room, trying by feel to find a spade. Finally, he struck a match. A pair of eyes blinked at him. Kangaroo rat. He found the tool he wanted, strode toward the knoll above the dry streambed. High ground, safe from flash floods. And, when the waters ran, a pleasant enough spot. He marked out two plots by moonlight, etching out rectangles in the earth, and began digging.

A half hour later, despite the cool, he was bare-backed. Sweat coursed down his back. Every so often, he stopped, listened for Tommy. He went to the kitchen for coffee twice. Tommy didn't stir, either time. It was quiet. A pack of coyotes yapped chromatically on a distant plateau. Another pack answered from one of the mesas. He missed the sounds of cattle, wondered if he'd ever get back to it again.

Captain Joe whinnied softly as Morgan passed his corral two hours later.

The graves were dug. Shallow. He went to the bunkhouse, where he had taken the body of Tío Pedro. He wrapped him in his blanket, struggled with the weight of the man. The air inside the adobe was sweet. The smell of death. He lugged the blanketed body to the far grave, lay it flat, faceup.

The sound of the dirt hitting the blanket made Morgan's gut tighten. He worked fast, then, shoveling the

36

gravel over the blanket, unable to look at the wrapped body anymore. It took him twenty minutes to pile large stones over the mound.

"*Adiós, Pedro,*" he said when he was finished. "*Vaya con Dios, amigo.*"

And that was the only prayer he could say for a man who had been a friend, a companion, part of the family. Tommy had loved him. So had Bonnie. But Tommy had never mentioned Tío Pedro this night. Perhaps he didn't want to know the truth—or knew it and didn't want to say it aloud and make it so.

Morgan put his shirt back on and walked back to the tackroom. The night was growing cooler and the forbidding silhouettes of the Little Dragoons stood out against the velvet star-speckled sky. It had taken him a long time to find such a valley and now it was spoiled, ruined by men who had taken the only thing he valued from him. Luke Trask had carried a grudge a long time—but the men with him were strangers. He didn't know any of them. Their names were unfamiliar.

He had known Trask was following him all these years. Now he regretted that he hadn't stayed long enough in one place to face him down. If he had killed him, maybe Bonnie would be alive now. Yet he had hoped all along that Trask would give it up, would come to realize that Ned had been wrong. Some men couldn't see the truth even when it stared them in the face. Ned was that way. Bonnie had never loved him. She liked him, true, but he had lost fair and square. Had he taken the loss like a man, he might be alive today, with another woman just as fair as Bonnie, just as good. At least with someone who loved him and someone he could love, as well.

Morgan shook his head. There was no explaining such things. If he'd killed Luke Trask, too, then people would have said he had killed Ned unfairly. But he should have killed Luke. And now he had to kill him. Bonnie had begged him. He had promised.

He would have to find someone to care for Tommy—if the boy healed. Right now it was touch and go. There was no way to know how bad his insides were hurt.

Chad went back inside the house. He stood at the door for a long time, sniffing the air, wondering where the men were now, the men who had torn his life to shreds, killed a part of him that could never be replaced. Out there somewhere in the hills. Watching the place? Gloating? Bragging about what they had done to Bonnie?

Morgan closed the door, a bitter taste in his mouth.

He locked it and wished he had a dog like so many ranchers did. A dog would give a warning if Trask came back in the night. Captain Joe might, or the horse Tío Pedro had been shoeing, Bonnie's horse, Patsy.

The house was empty, silent. He drank another cup of coffee, dampened the fire in the stove.

Tommy slept fitfully. Morgan undressed, lay on the bunk nearby. He stared at the dark ceiling for a long time, thinking. Tommy's breathing was audible. It was like a rasping board in a light wind. Scratching, scratching. Annoying. Frustrating.

He turned over, shut his eyes.

The sobs came then, hard and long and deep.

He let them come. Let them wash over him like a nighttide. Dark, cleansing, brutal.

In a while, he slept.

* * *

The men were giants.

They rode huge misshapen elephants, great bulging animals that blazed fire from their eyes, struck sparks with their hooves.

The men came at him from all directions. They shouted something he couldn't understand. They carried rifles that were as limber as whips.

Morgan ran, frightened.

He slogged through the thick mire of the nightmare, struggling to free his feet, to gather speed. A maze of twisted corrals blocked his way. He became lost. When he turned around, the elephants had disappeared, but a lone man, his face hidden in shadow, still stalked him. In his hand, a bright pistol glistened from five points, like a star. The pistol wriggled and grew into a snakelike object. A rope. It whirled over the man's head as he came closer, his arm twisting to widen the loop.

Morgan saw a little boy tumbling down a dark hill.

The boy did not look like Tommy, but it was Tommy. He was calling to him from faraway.

A woman rose up out of the earth. She was light-haired. It was Bonnie. Her face began to melt like candlewax, until it distorted into a hideous mask. The boy continued to tumble. Now he was screaming, "Mama! Mama!"

Morgan started running toward the boy. His feet left the ground and he sailed over the eerie nightscape of the dream, past twisted trees, over the man with the rope and the star-shaped pistol. He sailed on, higher and higher, trying to slow down. He flew toward a mass of light, a sky pulsing like flesh.

And, far off, he heard the boy screaming.

"Mama! Mama! Come back!"

Morgan jolted awake.

He blinked off shreds of dream, shook his head. His eyes swept the room.

Tommy's bed was empty!

"Mama! Wake up!"

The screams were muffled. It took Morgan a moment to get his bearings. He rubbed his eyes, jumped out of his bunk.

Tommy was in Bonnie's room. Morgan ran toward him, his heart squeezed, struggling in the cage of his chest.

His worst fears were realized when he saw Tommy atop his mother's bed, tears rivering down his face, shaking her.

Tommy looked at his father. "Mama won't wake up, Papa. She . . . she can't hear me."

Chad took his son in his arms, held him close. The boy was shivering, his fever raging. His forehead was hot, damp. Morgan squeezed his son gently, ran fingers through the boy's hair. "It's all right, Tommy. Don't cry anymore."

"What's the matter with Mama?"

Light smeared the morning sky outside the window. He looked at the boy, wondering how to tell him the truth, how to make him understand what death was, what it meant to him. "She . . . she's gone, Tommy. Gone to heaven."

"Is she dead?"

Surprised, Chad swallowed hard. "Yes, Son. She's dead."

"Won't she ever come alive?"

"No."

Tommy's face clouded up. He gasped for breath as a terrible convulsion shook his tiny body. He reached out a hand for his father. The breath wouldn't come. His face purpled, then faded to a pale blue.

"Don't Tommy!" Chad said. He shook the boy, trying to force air into his lungs. Tommy shook all over. His eyes rolled back in their sockets. Blood bubbled up in his mouth, spilled over onto his nightshirt. He gave a soft cry, shook one last time, and closed his eyes.

Chad wiped the boy's mouth of blood, tried to breathe air into his lungs. He laid him down on the bed, next to his mother, and pushed on his belly. There was no response.

"Tommy," he said quietly, "I love you. I love you so goddamned much, Son!"

And the tears came again as he picked the boy up in his arms, rocked him against his heaving, sob-wracked chest.

CHAPTER FIVE

Chad Morgan put the last stone on his son's grave, stood up. The sun was low in the sky, buttered behind scudding clouds. The morning haze had lifted and it was warm. That was why he had gotten the burying done early.

Tommy's small grave was next to his mother's. He'd wrapped the boy in his favorite blanket, tucked his stuffed squirrel in his arms. Bonnie had made that for him, sewing burlap over sawdust, buttons for eyes, hog bristles for whiskers, colored cloth for mouth and the pink insides of its ears. She had patched it more than once, stuffing fresh sawdust inside to keep its shape. Tommy would never go to sleep without Rusty in his arms.

Now the two would sleep forever.

Morgan took off his hat, said a silent prayer over the graves of his wife and son.

He walked back to the house slowly, carrying his hat.

Inside, he checked his saddlebags a final time. He

had searched high and low for something else: the wedding ring he had given Bonnie. She always wore it. It was gold, with a small diamond.

Ammunition for the .44-.40 Winchester, the Remington .44; jerky, hardtack, coffee, a small can to cook it in, flour, beans, a skillet, sulphur matches, a hatful of grain for Captain Joe—he and his horse didn't need much. His bedroll lay on the kitchen table next to the saddlebags. The canteens, both of them were full.

He hefted the items, stalked through the house, his boots ringing on the hardwood floors. He had hauled lumber from Santa Fe so that Bonnie wouldn't have a dirt floor like everybody else in that part of the country. His footsteps echoed hollowly in the dark, empty house. One of the men had taken Bonnie's ring, he was sure. It was a memento he wished he had now.

He shut the door, walked to the stables. He turned Patsy loose, saddled up Captain Joe. After slipping the Winchester in its scabbard, he slung canteens over the saddle horn and tied the bedroll on with thongs, aligned the saddlebags back of the cantle.

Morgan glanced once more at the three graves atop the hill. Later he would come back and put crosses over them. He'd dig a post hole, creosote the wood and set them deep and get someone to carve the names in, or burn 'em in. He'd seen some markers with nails making up the letters, but these rusted out in a hurry. Nothing lasted, but at least passersby would know their names for a time and how they died. After he left, he didn't care if anyone knew or not.

He rode to the creek, up the rise, following the tracks. They were not as fresh as he would have liked, but they would give him a direction. If it didn't rain, he might track the men a long way. He looked back at the ranch. It had his heart in it, his sweat. Could he come back to it after he had found the killers of his wife, son, and Tío Pedro? He didn't know. It was a good place, but lonesome without people to make it hum. When he saw Curly again, he'd talk about it.

He looked up at the sky. The buzzards were there, but high up over the little butte. He'd sprinkled some talc in the burial blankets, rose water in Bonnie's. The worst danger was the coyotes. He'd piled up enough stones to discourage them, he thought. He didn't want to think about that. When he got to a town, he'd have to send word to Bonnie's folks, the Lewises, back in Ellsworth. They'd want to know. They'd probably blame him, but it didn't matter. Bonnie wasn't close to them. His own folks were dead.

Morgan started riding again. He hitched his shoulders. Felt as if something was buried between the blades. It was a bad sign. He stopped, looked around the country.

Something was wrong. Nothing he could see, just a feeling. But a strong one. As if someone was watching him or following him. He turned around, looked back. He could barely see the top of the log-adobe house. He rode on, but the feeling persisted.

He found the place where the men had ridden up. Saw Tommy's small footprints in the red dust near a cedar tree. His hands grew clammy. The hairs on the back of his neck bristled. He swallowed the lump in his throat, forced himself to go on. Tommy's last hours had been terrible. A brutal thing had been done to him. No child should have to leave life in that manner: scared, hurt, confused. Morgan's jaw hardened as he thought about it. He would think about it for a long time.

Harley Matling crawled on his belly up to the rock. He stifled a sneeze as dust rose up in the air, filled his nostrils.

Fred Parsons crawled up beside him a moment later.

The two men had circled the ranch, found a butte behind the house about five hundred yards away. It afforded them a prime lookout. By being cautious, they would not be seen. Parsons had scouted it, set up the escape route if it became necessary.

Both men had rifles smeared with dust to keep the sun from bouncing off the metal.

"Reckon the kid bought it, too," Matling said.

"Near as I can make out, they's three graves down there."

"Tough on a man," Harley said.

Parsons slid a plug of Climax up his side, bit off a chaw. He tucked the wad in the side of his mouth, squeezed juice, spat.

"Trask wants it tough."

"But a little kid . . ."

"Nits make lice."

"Yair, I reckon."

The two men watched as Morgan walked down the hill from the graves, carrying his hat in his hand. They ducked low in case he looked up. He didn't.

They saw him head toward the corral.

A moment later, the black horse trotted out, began grazing on buffalo grass.

"He's turnin' out the other horse," Harley said.

Parsons squinted, saw that it was so. Morgan was out of sight at that moment, in the corral.

"You know anything about this jasper?" Harley asked.

Parsons shook his head. "Only that Luke Trask don't like him none."

"You hear what he was talkin' about to Higgins last evenin'?"

"Nope. Don't care. That there's a soddy down there what runs a little cattle. He ain't nothin' you ain't seen before up in Kansas, Missoura. Homesteader. The piss of the earth."

Matling started to laugh, but checked himself. He worked his rifle out from under him, off to the side. Too much movement would give them away. While they had the advantage, Trask didn't want them mixing if they didn't have to. It would be easy, though, to pick Morgan off from their vantage point.

"Here he comes," Parsons said.

"Be damned. Follerin' our tracks. That don't look like no soddy to me."

"Shut up, Harley."

They watched Morgan ride off toward the southwest. When he looked up at the buzzards, both men froze, held their breaths. He rode on, then stopped again. For a moment, Parsons was sure he was staring straight at them. He looked up, saw the buzzards circling high up in the air. He breathed a sigh of relief. He followed Morgan's look back to the three graves on the hill.

"He's moving funny," Parsons said. "Like somethin's botherin' him. Look."

Morgan was hesitating, looking down at the ground then back toward the ranch.

Then he rode on.

"Not much to tell Trask, is there?" Harley said. "He'll likely give up on the tracks. He'll lose the trail at the San Pedro."

"Umm." Fred Parsons wasn't so sure. "Mebbe he's thinkin' of comin' back, Harley. Let's make it mighty hard for him."

"Huh?" Harley rolled over, shaded his eyes from the sun, low in the eastern sky.

"Burn him out. So he's got nothin' to come back to. Trask might like that." Parsons grinned.

"Yeah, he might."

"We'll give him plenty of time. Likely he's got coal oil around for the lamps. I hate soddies. Bastards stake out every damn bit of unclaimed country, think they own everything in sight."

Harley was surprised at Parsons, his bitterness. The man was a homeless rake who had been on the owlhoot so long he was beginning to see better in the dark than in the daytime. That was probably why Parsons was always keen to raise hell in every little stickwood town they ever passed through. He was wont to pick a fight every time he saw someone wearing a pair of overalls or farmer's boots. It was something to keep in mind. He didn't know much about Parsons, nor any of the others, but you got to watching a man you rode with mighty careful, looking for clues to a past few seldom mentioned.

"Think Trask would want us to burn him out?" Harley asked.

"Hell, what difference does it make? He ain't comin' back. Trask may have wanted him to suffer some, but

47

if'n it comes to a face-off, Trask would just buy him a small plot of hard dirt."

"Yair, I reckon."

But Harley wasn't so sure. Trask never mentioned doing anything else but finding out what the jasper was up to, how he took his grief. He reckoned that Parsons being second in command was good enough reason to follow what he said. As long as Trask wasn't around.

"Come on, Harley, let's shinny down there and see how she burns."

There was no mistaking the glee in Parsons's voice. He scrambled to his feet, caught up his horse. He was like a kid going to see what the muskrat traps fetched up. Harley had to ride hard to catch up. They circled the butte and came pounding up to the ranch house in a cloud of rosy dust. Parsons hit the ground running, a strange light in his eyes. Harley swung down, too, his belly full of fluttering butterflies. It was spooky being around an empty house, with the ghosts of its dead lingering in the dry, still air.

Parsons kicked in the front door. His powerful impact split the leather of one hinge. The door hung at a crazy angle.

"Come on, Harley," he yelled. "Help me find the coal oil. We'll give 'er a good soakdown and put the match to 'er."

Harley went inside, but he didn't like it any.

Parsons was like a kid turned loose in a candy store. But Harley remembered what had happened in the house the day before. He didn't like ghosts.

"In here!" Parsons yelled. "Two jugs of coal oil and ever' damn lamp full."

Harley went into the kitchen. The fumes overpowered him. Parsons was slinging lamp oil in every direction.

"Jesus," Harley said. "Likely you'll go up with the house, you're not careful."

"Start breaking them lamps. In the front room, the bunk rooms. We're going to have a bonfire, sure 'nough."

The woman's bedroom didn't look the same. Drawers in the bureau pulled open, the doily on top mussed. The bloody bedsheets wadded up and tossed in a corner. Pillows stripped.

"Hey, Fred, take a look!" Harley called.

Parsons came in, carrying a half-empty glass jug of coal oil. He whistled. "Man sure as hell was a-lookin' for somethin'," he said. "You didn't take anythin', did you?"

Harley shook his head. "Trask took that weddin' ring off'n the woman's finger."

"Yair . . . Spread that lamp oil on the bed," Parsons said, pointing to the pair of hurricane lamps on the dresser. "Soak it good."

Matling took the chimneys out of the lamps, opened the fill holes, and sprinkled oil on the bed, floor, and curtains. Parsons poured oil around the base of the walls, left a trail to the door. Satisfied, he went to the front room and used up the rest of the bottle. Then, he smashed the lamps and hurled them at the walls.

"Better get out in the air," Parsons told Matling. "I'm ready to toss a match on the floor and run like Billy Hell."

Harley ran outside, caught up to the horses. He led them some distance from the house. Horses were peculiar around fire. If they were in the barn when it was afire, it was pure hell to get them out. They'd rather stay inside and burn than leave their stalls. It was some puzzling.

He watched as Parsons stood in the doorway, fumbled for a match. Parsons drew one out, struck it on the sole of his boot. The match flared. He tossed it inside and then stepped back a pace.

Nothing happened.

"Shit!" Parsons yelled.

He lit another match, tossed it inside the house. This time he stayed by the door and watched to see if it would catch.

Harley's mouth was dry. He looked around nervously as if to see if anyone was watching. He felt the same way he did when he was ten years old, playing with flint and tinder with some boys who lived near him in Missouri. The tinder had caught and he'd flung it into the barn. Then, he and the other boys had tried for ten minutes to find it. They'd finally given up and he'd gone off fishing with them. When they got back, the barn was gone. His pa had flayed his hide with a leather quirt and taken away his fishing pole for pretty near a year. He hadn't liked fires since.

Fire was bad medicine as far as Harley Matling was concerned. He'd seen a forest fire once that had burned clean across the border into Arkansas. It was some beautiful at night, but seeing the charred carcasses of deer and 'coons, of snapping turtles and rabbits, squirrels, had left him in awe of any conflagration of that size. The Morgan place was out in the open, not near timber, but Parsons's act was no less frightening to him.

Parsons turned and started running toward him. "She caught!" he yelled.

Matling saw smoke billowing out the front door. Thick, white. The stench of coal oil wafted on the draft of the smoke.

Harley stared at Parsons. The transformation was astounding. Fred's face shone with an inner light. His eyes glittered like multifaceted precious stones and the look on his face was one of pure rapture, as if he'd discovered gold or been given an expensive gift. As the smoke boiled out the front door, flames danced behind the windows, bright orange tongues that flicked at the wood, the furniture—anything that would burn.

The house seemed to draw a breath and then explode as gas pockets formed. Pieces of sod and log shot up in the air. The flames rose through the holes in the roof.

"Come on, Fred!" Harley yelled. "Let's get the hell out of here!"

"Jesus! Look at her burn!" Parsons drooled.

Another muffled explosion cracked the air.

The back door blew out. A stove lid sailed through the air, whistled like a high-speed bullet.

Smoke funneled out of a half-dozen openings, spiraled upward in the air until it became one long column. When it hit the upper air currents, it fanned out, spread in a T-shape over the single spire of fumes.

Parsons couldn't move. He was rooted to the earth, gazing at the conflagration with awe and admiration.

He didn't even hear Harley yelling at him. His body shuddered as if a current had passed through him.

At the crotch of his trousers, a damp stain appeared, slowly spread across the bulge. "Look at her," he rasped to no one. "Just look at her."

CHAPTER SIX

Chad Morgan jolted in his saddle when he heard the first explosion.

Captain Joe almost ran out from under him. His hindquarters dipped as he dug in with his rear hooves and skittered for ten yards before Morgan could rein him in.

"Ho, boy! Steady," he soothed.

Morgan swung the animal in a half-turn, stood up in the stirrups to gaze at his backtrail.

Moments later, a second explosion rocked the air.

Captain Joe backed up, nostrils flaring, eyes wide in fear.

Morgan eased him forward, prodding him in the flanks with the rowelless spurs.

That's when he saw the column of smoke. His eyes narrowed, his jaw twitched as tension triggered a long muscle, and the bottom dropped out of his stomach. The smoke could only be coming from one source. The ranch!

Trask!

Morgan sank back in the cradle of the saddle and rammed his spurs into Captain Joe's flanks. The horse's mane flowed in the wind as he streaked back toward the ranch. Sure-footed, he clattered over the trail, sparks flying from stones struck by his shod hooves. The animal deftly dodged stately saguaro, weaving in and out without any guidance from his rider. Cottonwoods flashed white against the deep red earth, then the green of cedars and scrub pines as man and horse raced toward the ranch just beyond the next rise.

As they crested the hill, Morgan saw the house afire. He saw something else, too . . .

Two men, one mounted, the other standing several yards from the house, shielding his face from the blazing heat.

Morgan jerked the Winchester from its scabbard, reined in hard.

Captain Joe skidded to a stop. His rider levered the rifle, jacking a shell into the firing chamber.

Morgan took quick aim, squeezed.

It seemed to take forever for the bullet to steam four hundred yards.

A puff of dust rose in the air just behind the man on foot. Morgan saw him turn and look up at him. Then, the man started running toward the riderless horse held by the mounted man. The man on the horse drew a pistol.

Morgan levered the empty casing out, heard the metallic click as the slide worked the other shell into the chamber. He swung the barrel, squeezed off a shot. High. The distance was deceptive. He was firing downhill and at an exorbitant range. The .44-.40 fried the air and he saw a chink fly out of the tackroom door just past the two men. They were both mounted now, and the running man had drawn his pistol. Orange flame and smoke belched from two pistols. Bullets whined as they spanged off rocks, whistled harmlessly off at tangents.

Not even close.

But the bastards were serious.

Morgan rammed the Winchester back into its scabbard, grabbed up the reins, and charged downslope. The two men emptied their pistols at him as Captain Joe zigzagged at Morgan's command of the reins. The horse leaped the dry streambed, started to eat up ground as the two men crammed fresh bullets into their pistols.

"Damn you, Fred, he came back!"

"Split up, Harley!" Parsons shouted. "He can only follow one of us. Whoever he goes after, the other one can take him from the rear. Now, ride!"

Morgan heard them shouting to each other as the distance closed to two hundred yards. Captain Joe slipped on one of the sharp turns and lost ground. The men separated, riding off in opposite directions.

Morgan didn't know which was which, but he had two names that matched those Bonnie had told him. Fred would be Fred Parsons. Harley would be Harley Matling. Where was Trask? The man named Higgins? From the tone of their voices and from what they said, he had a hunch Trask was nowhere around. Higgins probably wasn't, either. Why had these two come back? To burn him out? To finish the job? It didn't make sense. Trask would have wanted to kill him personally. Instead, these two were trying to match up bullets in their guns with his hide, his name.

55

The two men rode fast over level ground. Captain Joe was winded from the long ride, showed the strain as he raced up the gentle slope rising from the stream-bed. Smoke obscured Morgan's vision momentarily. He listened for the sound of hoofbeats to get his bearings. All he could hear was the roar and crackle of the fire. The house was a blazing inferno, the fire fed by lamp oil and furniture. He felt the heat as he swung left.

He couldn't chase both men at once. Morgan made his choice. The one who had ridden to the left would be the easiest. The direction he had taken would lead him through a series of arroyos and dry gulches, over rough ground. Unless he swung back south, he would be trapped in a box canyon. If he went north, the country got worse. The man riding east would run into the mountains unless he, too, swung south.

Morgan emerged from the smoke, saw the man he was after some five hundred yards ahead and pulling away. His horse was fresh, while Captain Joe was winded. Morgan's side ached from the exertion, but he knew it would go away once he got his second wind. Captain Joe, however, would have to be eased up soon, before he foundered.

Instead of following his man on a direct course, Morgan angled to the south so that the man he was chasing would have to head west or north. He stayed in plain view, making certain the man would know he was being followed. There was no trace of the other one, who had ridden east. Smoke obscured his vision in that direction. It would also help his case, since the other man couldn't see him, either.

Morgan eased up on Captain Joe. The horse slowed to a walk. His coat gleamed with sweat. He had not yet started to lather and his breathing was clear. With rest, he would be fresh in a while. There was no hurry now, anyway. Whoever Morgan was following would have to hold up soon, too. He had pushed his mount pretty hard. A mile at that pace would begin to tell. More than that could cause the horse to go down.

The stabbing ache in his side began to diminish, fade away. Morgan took a deep breath, rocked in the saddle as Captain Joe found a comfortable gait. He took off his hat, wiped the sweatband. He swept a bandanna across his face, sopping up sweat. The sun was climbing now, hammering down on the land with a vengeance. If the man he was pursuing didn't have water, he was in for a hell of a day. The land ahead was dry, a maze of gullies, arroyos, blind canyons, and rugged terrain. Saguaros, each one different, studded the landscape.

Captain Joe shied at a Gila monster lying like a lump across the path, its forked tongue flicking in and out of its mouth. Morgan gave the horse his head, let him sidestep the strange beast. Lizards blinked in the sun and a hawk floated in the distance, low, hunting. The man ahead grew smaller and smaller, but he did not turn south. Instead, he angled off northwest.

Morgan cracked a grim smile.

He wondered which man he was following. It didn't make any difference. But, if he could, he wanted him alive. There were things he had to know and the man ahead could tell him, if he would.

He glanced over his shoulder. There was still no sign of the other man. But he would doubtless circle and try to get him in the back. To avoid being surprised, Morgan rode behind a ridge. That would give him some advantage—for a time. He could not afford to lose sight of the man ahead for long, however. He kicked Captain Joe into a faster jog, swinging now to the north.

Harley Matling slowed his horse. Morgan saw him stop and look back. Heat shimmered over the boiling land. Waves of light danced between the two men, hunter and prey. The distance between them was deceptive, but Morgan figured his man was almost two miles ahead. A goodly piece. It would be difficult to close the gap if he gave the man and his horse much chance to rest. He had to keep the pressure on; keep the man moving toward the box canyon. From there, he would have no escape. He would have to stand and fight.

"Get on, Captain Joe," Morgan said. The horse picked up speed.

Let the man know he's being chased, thought Morgan, angling toward the rider ahead.

Matling looked back. Morgan saw him slap his horse's rump with the tail ends of the reins.

"Work him to death, man," Morgan said aloud. "Run him into the ground."

Morgan slowed Captain Joe once he had his prey moving again. He stood up in the stirrups, leaned over the saddle horn, and looked back toward the ranch. The sky was filled with a pall of smoke hanging over the place that once was his home. He saw no sign of the other man. It was beginning to worry him— whether the man was smart or had decided to abandon his companion. There was no telltale smudge of dust on the horizon, so the man was moving slowly, in whatever direction he was headed.

An hour slipped by. Then another. The sun beat down mercilessly. Morgan's shirt stuck to his body, drenched with sweat. He tied the bandanna around his forehead, let it soak up the moisture instead of the hatband. His blue eyes squinted from the hard glare. He pulled his Stetson's brim low over his face then shifted it over the back of his neck as the sun crawled higher and started dropping toward afternoon. He chewed on jerky, a chunk of hardtack. He drank a quart of water from the canteen, cooled by evaporation.

The man he tracked was less than a mile ahead.

The distance lessened with each hour. Morgan had not let the man stop—not to piss, to drink, to rest his horse. Nor had he stopped. Instead, he seemed made of iron. The sun only served to temper his hardness. He rested Captain Joe by walking him fifteen minutes out of every hour. He ran him for a quarter mile, then let him canter for another thirteen hundred feet or so. Then trot, then a slow gallop. Varying the speeds. Never the same sequence. Push. Drive. Move the man ahead up into what would look like a wide clear valley with plenty of room.

It would look that way, but the "valley" took a dog-leg left and when the man turned there he would face a wall.

A box canyon!

Morgan stopped once, filled his hat with water after he swung down out of the saddle. Captain Joe buried his muzzle in the water, sucked it up through smacking lips. Morgan was back in the saddle again without the man ahead even knowing he had stopped. He performed the act in a shady draw that dipped below a ridge. When he reappeared, the man ahead was closer by an eighth of a mile. Morgan started crowding him then, edging him toward the box canyon. It was either that or face the badlands to the south. The country was dotted with buttes, plateaus, rock spires, cactus, lizards, rabbits, and snakes.

Freshened, Captain Joe responded to the new pace eagerly.

Morgan started closing the gap steadily.

The man looked over his shoulder often now. Morgan saw him kick his horse and rein-slap him. He got little response. The horse was tiring—pushed almost to the limit of its endurance. The heat, the miles, the lack of water, were all taking their toll on man and animal. Still Morgan pressed on, pushing, narrowing the distance, driving the man ahead of him over gradually flattening terrain.

Soon, Morgan knew, he would have to make a stand, either by choice or necessity.

The man was smart. He hadn't tried to circle or ambush Morgan. If he had, it would have been all over in a hurry. Morgan knew the country. It was obvious that the man he trailed did not. He could have made a stand, but it would then have been only a matter of time, with Morgan stalking, the other man held to a fixed position, unsure of where his enemy was, from what direction he would strike.

The box canyon loomed ahead. It was a natural place to ride for, and the man he trailed didn't disappoint him.

It looked like the road to freedom. The ridges started out low, then rose gradually. It appeared they would drop off again on the other side. There, a man might reason, would be a perfect spot for ambush.

Morgan suppressed a grin as Matling kicked his horse toward the entrance to the canyon.

He hauled up short, drew the Winchester from its sheath. Levering a shell into the chamber, he aimed high and fired at the man riding into the canyon. The bullet might carry. It would take a hell of a drop at that yardage. It would take some seconds for the report to reach him, but the man would know he was being pressed.

A spout of dirt kicked up a hundred yards behind the man.

Morgan saw him turn. The bullet struck before the sound of the cracking rifle reached him. He whacked his horse and rode deeper into the canyon—into the trap.

Morgan watched him go, sheathed the Winchester, and prodded Captain Joe into a rolling gallop. The distance between the two men lessened. Captain Joe gobbled up the yards with a long, smooth stride. He was rested, full of ginger again.

He didn't want the man to get too far ahead now. He might figure things out and, once he turned the bend, he'd have a slight advantage. If he was smart, he could hop off his mount, take cover behind the outcropping of rock. He might get off a shot or two, but there was no escape. He could either be starved out or driven back against the wall, in time.

Once, when Morgan looked back just before entering the canyon, he thought he saw something behind him. Or someone. It was movement. Dark and big. He strained his eyes to see better, but the shape was gone, swallowed up in the glaring sunlight, by the deep water scars in the rugged land. He rode on but knew he didn't have much time.

The other man was following him, he was sure. A long ways off, but back there—and coming on at a steady pace.

The man ahead slowed his horse.

Morgan urged Captain Joe on. The horse picked up speed.

The distance between the two men shrank.

Matling drew his rifle from its boot, sent a shot in Morgan's direction. Close enough to hear the angry whine as the bullet sizzled through the air, caromed off a rock. Morgan ignored it and pressed harder. Captain Joe got his legs under him, racing now, the wind in his teeth, mane flying, tail straight back like a dark and ragged flag.

The man rammed his rifle back in its sheath, wheeled, and started riding deeper into the canyon.

In a few minutes he would make the bend.

Then he would know.

Morgan came on, relentless. He saw the man make the turn. Morgan was close enough to see his face.

Two minutes later, Morgan turned into the box. He slowed Captain Joe. Took the turn in a walk.

The man was there, in the open. Waiting.

Morgan pulled up, eyed him. No weapon showing. The man had made his choice. He knew he had been suckered.

"Which one are you?" Morgan called across the two hundred yards separating the men. "Parsons or Matling?"

His words echoed in the canyon, bouncing off the walls, carrying to the high rocks, where they were swallowed up in a terrible muffling silence.

CHAPTER SEVEN

"I'm Harley Matling, Morgan!"

Matling's horse stood there, his head drooping to the ground, standing hipshot.

Morgan spurred Captain into a slow walk toward the man and his worn-out horse. As he rode, he reached into his pocket, found the two balls of cotton. He stuffed one wad in his left ear. He shifted the reins to his left hand. His other hand hung loose at his side, scant inches from the butt of his .44 Remington.

Matling saw what Morgan did, looked at him with puzzlement spreading across his face.

"What the hell you doing?" he shouted.

Morgan laughed mirthlessly. "Cotton in my ears, son. Gun noise bothers me."

"You . . . you're crazy, Morgan!"

Morgan said nothing. He kept coming on, slow. Ready, if Matling went for it.

"You got me cold, Morgan," Matling said. "Wasn't my idea, that fire. My horse is nigh done in and I've not much fight in me."

"You're one of Trask's bunch. That's enough."

"Figgered so. Any chance to palaver?"

Morgan knew the man was stalling for time. Waiting for Parsons to catch up, no doubt. If that shadow he'd seen back there was Parsons, they had a good quarter hour, maybe more, before he reached them.

The bearded man sat in his saddle, a lump of heavy flesh. His clothes were sodden with sweat. Pistols hung from his saddle horn, close enough to reach. He had a pair of them, one on either side of the horse, still another on his leg. If Matling was fast enough, he might ride out a winner.

"You talk, Matling. Tell me about my wife. My little boy."

Behind his beard, Matling's face drained of color. "I wasn't in on that," he lied.

Morgan knew he was lying. Bonnie had named their names: Trask, Matling, Parsons, and Higgins. She was dying when she told him. She didn't just make up the names. No, Matling was trying to save his skin.

The distance was closing.

A hundred yards.

Fifty.

Go for it, you sonofabitch! Morgan thought.

Matling had a lot of firepower showing. Most men took a lifetime to become proficient with just one pistol. One pistol in one hand. Matling may have been the exception. He might be able to bring two into play at once. Some men could, Morgan had heard. He had never seen such a man. A handgun was not much of a weapon except at very close range. And a man had to have time to aim, adjust his sighting, fire.

Forty yards. And still Morgan came on.

A cool-headed man might shoot well at that range. He might even kill. Yet the odds were against such a shot. If Matling tried it, the distance would be to Morgan's advantage. He could move, Matling could not, unless he left his horse. If the man went for two pistols, that would eat up much time . . . too much time.

Thirty-five yards.

Matling's hands rested on the pommel, palms shaped to the curve of the leather covering the wood. He might go for two pistols.

Morgan watched him closely for any movement—a shift of his eyes, the flick of a hand. His blue eyes bored into the puffy slits of Matling's porcine eyes, looking for any sign that the man was going to run or fight.

Thirty yards.

Close enough to smell the sweat on the man, see the sleek hide of his horse, its head still drooping, its chest heaving, breath rasping inside. Matling didn't move. But Morgan could see that the man was hunched, sitting solid, braced, feet firm in the stirrups, pushing against them. His body was rigid, shoulders relaxed and tilted slightly forward. His pistols just a split second away in oiled holsters.

Twenty-five yards.

Matling might not even have to draw. Morgan saw the cutaway holsters dripping from gunbelts slung on the saddle horn. All the man would have to do would be to hammer back and tilt the holster up, fire through the barrel hole.

Twenty yards away. Captain sidled left at Morgan's laying on of the reins. No protection from the horse

66

any more. Coming in broadside. But it would be easier to draw and shoot. Protection be damned.

"Morgan, back off. No need for you to take me on. Trask's the one with the grudge."

Morgan kept coming.

"I got a grudge, too, Matling."

Matling blinked his eyes.

Fifteen yards between the two men.

A dozen.

Morgan gentled Captain to a halt.

The two men faced each other in the blazing sun, each with his own thoughts. Each with his own plan of action. Captain snorted, raked a forefoot across the baked earth. Morgan stared at his quarry, wondering what kind of man would do what he had done—rape another man's wife, torture a small boy, murder a man, and set fire to a man's home.

He fought down the bile that threatened to surge up his throat, gag him. His stomach churned with hatred. Inside, he was seething, but he appeared calm, self-possessed.

Matling's eyes were a pair of puffed slits as he stared into the sun. His lips were dry, cracked, the rivulets turning white from the salt in his system. Dried blood stuck to the hairs of his beard just below his lips. Red dust streaked his face, islands divided by the drip-lines of sweat that coursed from his hairline to his neck. Fresh sweat on his cheeks and sideburns glistened silver in the sun. His brow dripped sweat, but he made no move to wipe the droplets away.

It might be the last move he would ever make.

"You got a lot of life left," Matling said, for openers.

"You can hunt down Trask if you want, or just go on and pick up someplace else."

"What about you, Matling? Can you live with my shadow? Someone always on your trail? Better to face it now than later on."

"Look, kid, I maybe made a mistake. Ridin' with Trask and all. Him and me are split up. He goes his way, I go mine. It's hot. I'm dog-assed tired and I got no quarrel with you, personally."

"Yair, you do, Matling. I want to see you go for it. You're pretty good with women, kids, and old men. How do you stand up to someone who can call you, card for card?"

"Shit, Morgan. I got sixty, eighty pounds on you. And a lot more gun."

"Talk is about as cheap as anything else out here, son."

Matling turned his head sideways as if to dismiss this upstart who was calling him out. It was a trick he had used to his advantage before. He shrugged as if giving up the conversation, the quarrel.

Morgan was not deceived.

A moment ticked by. That flick of an eyelash was as long as eternity.

Matling moved.

His hands, lightning quick, stabbed for his pistols. His body held as steady as a boulder in a wind. His eyes opened wide, flashed a quick fire. Supple hands, deceptively clumsy, grasped twin pistol butts. Twin thumbs pushed down on twin hammers. Pistols swung up, still in their holsters. Fingers curled around triggers.

Morgan's hand flew like a swift shadow to his pistol butt.

The jerk was clean, smooth as a trout leaping to an airbound fly. He hammered back as his gun cleared the leather. The trigger squeeze came as soon as the barrel's snout had locked in on its target.

The .44 bucked in Morgan's hand. A shade faster than Matling's twin blasts.

The air shattered with explosions. Smoke belched out of three pistol barrels. Hot lead fried the atmosphere. Echoes of the gunshots boomed through the canyon, faded into silence.

As soon as Morgan fired, he twisted out of the saddle, landed on his feet, Captain providing cover. Ducking under his neck, he snapped off another shot. Echoes rippled across rocky distances, bounced from the walls and steep cliffs.

The first of Morgan's bullets ripped into Matling's shoulder, snapping the collarbone, gouging out chunks of flesh. The man's scream followed the jolting impact of the heavy-grained bullet. Morgan's second shot cleared Matling out of the saddle, buckling him at the waist as it plowed through his gut, exploding stomach and guts into a pulpy bloody mass.

Matling landed on his rump, his belly leaking onto his lap. Chad Morgan ran to him, his pistol still smoking.

He hammered back, shoved the snout under Matling's nose. Matling's eyes frosted over, taking on the cast of imminent death.

"You haven't got long, son," Morgan told him. "I want to know two things from you. Your time gets longer as you talk."

"Jesus, I hurt," Harley groaned.

Morgan's finger tightened on the trigger. "You can go now," he said. "Or make your peace real quick. You're just a hair away from having no face at your funeral."

Panic flared in Matling's glazed eyes. "God, man, help me," he rasped. "Anything—I'll tell you any damn thing!"

"Where's Trask?" Morgan asked, taking the cotton from his ears.

"Tombstone. Christ, I'm burning up. My guts're on fire."

"Who took her ring?"

"Huh?"

Morgan rammed the barrel into Matling's upper lip. The man cringed in pain, shrank back. His hands came away from his belly, slimy with blood.

Matling started to slide away. Morgan grabbed his collar, held him up. The man's eyes rolled out of focus. He hadn't much time. Less than either of them knew.

"The ring. My wife's ring," Morgan charged. "Who took it?"

"Ring? Little ring? Pretty stones?"

Matling slipped even farther away, his eyes paling with the frozen glaze of death.

Morgan shook him hard. "Yes, Matling. The ring, dammit! Who took it?"

Matling's eyes struggled to focus. Morgan saw the pupils contract, then widen.

"T—Trask. He's got it."

A pair of prairie swifts darted past a saguaro, knifing through the air with dashing speed. A buzzard sailed in the distance, wafting on pinioned wings with the currents, sailing toward the two men, head swinging from side to side, keen eyes searching what his nostrils scented. It was quiet. The smell of black powder hung in the still air, thick as swamp ooze.

Matling's life ebbed away with each feeble pump of his heart.

He held up a hand to Morgan.

"Higgins," he muttered. "Higgins is the one to watch. Him and Trask . . ."

Morgan leaned down to hear what Matling was saying. The dying man made a gurgling sound. His eyes fluttered and closed. Then his body twitched for the last time.

"Captain Joe," Morgan called.

The big horse perked its ears, loped over to him with a lazy gait. Morgan mounted and shoved fresh shells in his pistol.

The world was ugly at that moment. He didn't like killing—for whatever reason. Or did he? Death wore a terrible face, no matter who it sought. He thought of Bonnie and of Tommy, of Tío Pedro. They didn't want to die. And they had died horribly. They had died without justice and without reason and without sense. They had died without a chance to live, to fight back, to protest. They had died at the hands of brutal men. They had died in the horror of mental and bodily torture. And that was the worst death of all.

Tommy's last moments were agonizing for him. A child, a boy of four summers, crushed to death like a flower trampled underfoot. Bonnie's last moments, too, were clouded by pain and the horror of what the men had done to her. And Tío Pedro, a good man, trying to help, shot down like a stray cur, beheaded like a chicken with a single shattering bullet that blotted out all thought, all past, present, and future.

Why?

Morgan clenched his fist, glared at the sky.

"Why!" he screamed.

Whywhywhywhywhywhy, the echo reverberated. *Whywhywhy. Whywhy.*

The silence crowded in on him. The scent of death clogged his nostrils. He climbed slowly up in the saddle. He looked for Matling's horse, saw it grazing a few hundred yards away. He rode toward it, caught up its reins. He climbed down from Captain, stripped the loose animal of saddle, blanket, bridle. Let it run free.

He rode out of the canyon, alert to danger. Matling's horse raced ahead, away from the stench of death.

Sunlight bounced off something metal just ahead.

Morgan slipped off to the side of Captain, hung on to the saddle horn.

A split second later, a thundering explosion roared into the silence.

A nearby rock trembled, shattered as the bullet struck it, caromed off with a ring-whine ricochet.

Morgan raced toward the white smoke hanging in the air, hanging on the plains Indian-fashion, his pistol already in his hand.

Parsons had made his play!

CHAPTER EIGHT

Jack Garth rubbed a slender hand across his bald pate. The fuzz was starting to grow back. He liked the feel of it, downy soft, stiff with stimulating electricity when he rubbed his hand across the fine hairs. He leaned against one of the porch posts of the Lone Wolf Saloon & Boarding House at the far end of Fremont Street. His pale-blue eyes swept the almost deserted street. That's where the nervousness showed—in his cold, almost colorless eyes.

Only twenty-four years old, some said Garth was full of tics that didn't show except when he thought no one was looking at him. And people looked at him a lot. He was striking in appearance. With not a full-grown hair on his head, an almost girllike slenderness to his frame, dark tight-fitting clothes, a height of almost six feet, he did not appear to be the average cowboy. He wore a battered Colt .45 low on his hip, the bluing gone, the barrel pitted from corrosion and use. Under his belt he carried a pocket Derringer, double-barreled. Handy, but out of sight. Some said he shaved his head because his folks had lost their hair to the Cheyenne when he was a pup. Others said he had come within an inch of being scalped by a band of Paiutes. The truth was somewhere in between. He had seen a family, like his own, slaughtered by raiding Apaches, scalped and mutilated. The shock was so great that his hair started to turn gray at eighteen. So, a combination of fear and anxiety about looking old had caused him to shave off his hair and keep it that way all these years.

"Curly," a voice behind him called, "the vittles is on."

Garth jumped and whirled, his pale eyes vacuous, deadly. "You bastard, Rudy, don't ever come up ahind me like that," he said with anger.

Rudy Owens gulped, finished tucking his shirttail in his trousers. Rudy was twenty. A shock of cowlick hair jutted out from his oversize sombrero, like scarecrow wheat. He had close-set eyes that were a nose shy of being crossed, a receding chin, long neck, and drooping shoulders that emphasized his long arms.

"Steve said to get you afore the steak loses its steam." Rudy looked sheepishly at Curly's right hand, deadly close to the butt of the .45. "Didn't mean to jump you," he apologized. "I'm hungry as a bear. You still lookin' fer somebody?"

Curly gave him a look of raw disgust. "Let's get on them steaks," he said.

Steve McCurdy served breakfast in the saloon. It was a second-rate place, with rooms in back and upstairs. Steve didn't care who stayed there as long as they paid in advance. It had started out as an adobe cantina and he'd bought out the Mexican who owned it, added another floor and a section in the rear. He'd put in a lot

74

of doors, a rear stairs. There was a boarding stable out back, and the men who stayed there could always find a fast way to exit if it became necessary. Steve kept some girls in a separate adobe back of the stables, and the path to its door was well worn.

Rudy and Curly made their way to a back room near the modest kitchen. A Mexican woman served them steaming platters of steak, corn cakes, biscuits, and *juevos rancheros* smothered in *salsa casera*. They drank mugs of hot, bitter coffee as they wolfed down their breakfasts. It was quiet; there were no other diners at that hour. Curly said little, but kept glancing toward the door, a muscle in his lean face twitching every time he did so.

"Expectin' someone?" Rudy asked as he mopped up the steak juices with a fluffy biscuit.

"Maybe," Curly said, leaning back to roll a quirly.

"You been jumpy as a cat in a roomful of rockin' chairs ever since yesterday."

"I got my reasons." Garth lit his cigarette, drew smoke into his lungs.

"You reckon Morgan got back all right?"

Curly fixed the youth with a piercing look. "Now, why would you ask that?"

Rudy shrugged, swallowed a sopping chunk of biscuit. It took him a moment to chew it down so he could reply. "No reason. I know he was anxious to get back to that purty wife of his."

Curly scowled. "Well, that's no never mind. We done our job for him and he won't be building no herd anytime soon."

"I hear tell Ringo's down to Bisbee. Curly Bill Brocius is in town, which Wyatt Earp don't like none too well . . ."

Curly interrupted him with a sarcastic sneer in his voice.

"Well now, you're just a reg'lar gossip, ain't you, Rudy? I don't give a damn about Ringo or none of them others."

Rudy Owens got on his nerves. He had the irritating habit of always saying the wrong thing at the wrong time or bothering a man when he wanted to be alone. He was a good kid, but he didn't know which side his bread was buttered on. The truth was that Johnny Ringo was one of Curly's heroes. He had tried to hook up with him and had been given the cold shoulder. Same with Curly Bill Brocius, who had laughed him down, told him to get a wig on his bald pate. The humiliation had stung and hurt deep.

The doorway darkened.

Luke Trask filled the frame. He looked at Curly, ignoring Rudy Owens.

Curly's face went chalk. He quickly recovered his composure and started to rise from his chair.

Trask waved him back down. "Just rode in," he said. "Meet you out at the bar. Take your time."

Trask turned and was gone. Curly doused the quirly in his plate. "You get scarce, Rudy," he said. "I got business."

"Ain't that—"

"Rudy, don't go mixin' in." Curly tossed a cartwheel on the table, got up. "You go on and hook up with someone. Evers might need hands."

"Ain't we—"

"No, we ain't. You tell the others to look out for theirselfs."

With that, Curly left the room. Rudy stared at him, shrugged, went back to the dregs on his plate.

Trask was looking at a copy of the *Epitaph*, a bottle of whiskey on the table, a half-full glass of Old Overholt next to it. Curly saw that his eyes were rheumig from lack of sleep, his beard untrimmed. He couldn't have been in town long. Curly looked around the saloon to see if the other boys were there. Trask was alone. The barkeep, husband of the cook, had the morning duty. Mostly his job was to clean up the glasses left by the night barkeep and to clean off all the shelves, polish the bar, and take care of customers. Curly knew him only as Nuñez. Beyond that, he didn't care much.

"Sit down, Curly," Trask said, hissing through a matchstick stuck between his teeth.

Curly sat down. "Anything new?" he asked.

Trask laughed drily, worried the match to the other side of his mouth. "You did good, Curly. I owe you. The timing was right."

"Wha—what did you do?" the bald-pated man whispered as he leaned over the table.

"Whiskey? This is prime. None of that Taos lightning."

"Ah, too early for me. I just finished breakfast."

"Me 'n Higgins been ridin' all night. Broke fast at Benson afore dawn. Got some knots unkinked."

"Where's Harley and Fred?"

Trask thumbed over his shoulder. "They're a-comin'. Stayed behind to assess the damages." Trask reached into his pocket, took out a small roll of bills. He shoved them across the table to Curly. "Here's what I owe you."

Curly didn't touch the roll. He stared at it, then at Trask.

"Go on, take it. You earned it."

"What about Morgan?"

"Oh, Harley and Fred'll be along directly. Morgan's got a lot to think about, I reckon."

"Did you . . . Did she . . . I mean . . ."

"You mean was his woman there? She was and she got taken care of real good. Now, there's your money, Curly. And you're in the clear."

Curly picked up the money and idly counted it. It was all there. Thirty dollars.

"I'll accept the money, but you know what I really want, Trask."

Trask extracted the matchstick from his mouth, finished off the glass of whiskey. He closed his eyes as if savoring the heat. For a moment, Curly thought he was falling asleep in his chair. But Trask shook his big frame and opened his eyes.

He rubbed the bridge of his nose as if in pain. "Curly," he said finally, "you got ambition. I know you tried to get on with Johnny Ringo and that bunch. And that Bill Brocius turned you down flat. Well, I appreciate you wanting to jine up with me. And I'll give you some good advice: count yourself lucky you ain't in with that bunch, 'cause they're all one now. Earp is all family and he won't have any outsiders. The Clantons is finished, 'cept for that yellowback Ike and his no-account kin. So that leaves only me and my bunch. At the moment, we're full up, and that's the truth."

"But I can't make no money herdin' beeves! And I got a lot to learn. But how in hell can I learn it if'n nobody'll give me the chance?"

"Don't whine, Curly. I don't like whinin'."

"Sorry."

"One thing about you is that you stand out. Let your hair grow back. Gray or black, it don't make no difference. And start wearin' ordinary clothes. If you don't like your gray hair then put some black boot polish on it and wear a big hat. Me and my bunch don't chunk no rocks in the lake so we don't make no ripples. We live quiet and we talk polite around the starpackers."

"I know. You're the best, Trask. You don't have to convince me."

"This ain't no advertisement, Curly. Ever wonder why we get along? Well, if I ever take you on, I'll maybe tell you. But you got something to chaw on for a while and we'll leave it at that."

Curly started to say something but decided against it. At least Trask had left the door open and that was something. There was still hope.

Trask reached into his vest pocket and took out Bonnie's ring. He held it to the light, squinting at its tiny sparkles.

Curly's mouth dropped open. "Why, that's . . ."

Trask grinned. "Pretty, ain't it?"

"I admired it a time or two. Did Miz Bonnie give it to you?"

Trask threw back his shaggy head and roared with laughter. The laugh was hollow in the almost empty room. Rudy Owens came out to see what was happening, then returned without saying anything. His boots rang on the hardwood floors as he continued past the dining room to the hall that led to his own room.

"She give me more'n that," Trask guffawed. "A sight more."

"You didn't—"

"Now, Curly, don't fret yourself about what we did or didn't do. We done what was offered to us to do and that was that."

Curly looked at Trask with renewed interest. When he had agreed to tell the outlaw that Morgan would be gone during a certain time period, he hadn't asked why. It had something to do with an old grudge. Yet, if Trask had gone there when Morgan was still at Fort Huachuca, then he must have done something bad to his wife, too. Maybe to the kid, as well. Curly wondered if he'd ever find out just what did happen at Morgan's ranch.

"What're you going to do with that . . . with her ring?"

"Why? You want to buy it?"

"I might. There's a girl I'm pretty sweet on. If'n I had a ring like that, she just might—"

"Might drop her britches for you, eh, Curly?"

Curly flushed. Trask poured another drink. He was about three sheets to the wind as it was, Curly thought. Either he had drunk too much or been without sleep too long. Or both.

"Well, she . . . she's a virgin, I guess."

"Haw!" Trask slapped his ham of a leg and roared with laughter again. "Hell, if she's a virgin, I'll give you the damn pretty. But if she ain't, I want fifty bucks on the barrelhead."

"I'll give you fifty for it now," Curly said, uneasy.

He didn't know whether Trask was funning him or not. He just felt uncomfortable.

"Hell, you got a deal, *'chacho*. Fork it on over."

Curly gave Trask the thirty dollars back and a double eagle besides. He still had money left and some saved up. But he didn't want to go back to working for wages again.

Since the silver strike a couple of years before, when Ed Schieffelin stumbled over the richest strike in frontier history as he was poking his pick into the mountain slopes east of the San Pedro Valley, everyone had money except a few hard-luck cases like himself. It was Schieffelin who had called his staked claim "Tombstone." Since then, the town had drawn every thief and cutthroat in the West to its maw. Silver, assaying at twenty thousand dollars a ton, became the chief preoccupation of hard-luck prospectors, robbers, bankers, merchants, and gamblers. Tombstone boomed. A stageline was established between Tucson and Tombstone, bringing in freight and people. The whores came in the first flood and set up in cribs along Allen Street and a few on Fremont. Tombstone was a wide-open city and it hadn't changed much since 1878 when Schieffelin had cracked open the first vein of silver.

Trask kissed the ring and handed it to Curly.

Nuñez looked at the two curiously as he mopped the bar to a high sheen.

Curly put the ring deep inside his pocket. He grinned wide. "Maybe I'll have that drink now," he said.

"Nuñez, bring another glass," Trask ordered.

The sound of boots clumping on the porch drew the men's attention to the door.

"Make that two glasses," Trask said.

"*Sí, señor,*" assented the barkeep.

A nervous young man with fresh-cut short blond hair came through the batwing doors. Spittle bubbled at the corners of his mouth. He wore new clothes that fit him loosely. On his vest, a deputy's star shone bright. His large-roweled spurs jingled as he walked toward the table.

"Uh-oh," Curly breathed.

"Set a chair," Trask beamed. "Deputy Delbert Harris, ain't it?"

The young man nodded, smiled weakly.

"Shake hands with Curly Garth, Deputy."

Deputy Harris shook Garth's hand as he sat down. He pushed his new Stetson back, stretched out his legs adorned with kidskin half-boots. "I just got sworn in a half hour ago," Harris said.

"Now we're all set," said Trask. "Morgan will have a hard way to go if he comes to Tombstone."

Curly was puzzled. Something was going on he didn't understand. Trask poured three drinks, raised his glass in a toast.

"Here's to law and order," he said.

"Yeah," said Delbert Harris, who had formerly gone by the name of Dave Higgins.

The men drank. Harris and Trask laughed until their eyes ran with tears.

Curly felt a tightening in his gut that he couldn't explain.

CHAPTER NINE

Morgan pulled himself back up in the saddle after the sixth shot. There was a good chance that Parsons would have to reload—unless he wanted to empty his rifle and take the chance that Morgan would run him down.

Smoke hung in clusters from a clump of rocks off to the right. Morgan's ears rang with the booming repercussions of the explosions. He saw Parsons scrambling down from the rocks, disappearing over the other side.

Morgan drew up, shoved his pistol back in its holster. Quickly, he stuck cotton balls in both ears, drew the Winchester from its scabbard. He approached the rocks warily, cocking as he rode. A fresh shell slid into the magazine with a harsh metallic sound.

A horrible cry reached his ears, muffled. A shriek of pain that was almost human. Just ahead, in a shallow gully, he saw Matling's horse. It was down on its side, its legs sawing the air freely. Its neck and belly ran with bright ribbons of blood, a crimson sash girdled its flanks. It had caught at least two, possibly three, bullets. The horse's eyes rolled when he rode up, and again there was that terrible near-human bleating. Morgan threw down on the animal, squeezed the shot off without thinking. The horse's forehead twitched. Dust flew out of its hide. It thrashed a few more times and then was still; out of its misery.

It was hell, killing a big animal like that. But the horse was in mortal pain and there was no reason for it to suffer needlessly.

Besides, the horse had most likely saved Morgan's life running between him and the bushwhacker. He owed Matling one if they ever met up in some dark or shining beyond. The man had been good for something, even if he had to die first.

Morgan turned away. He kept seeing little Tommy's face, the pain in his eyes. Kept hearing his screams when his mother wouldn't wake up.

Parsons!

He must know now that Matling wasn't coming out!

Morgan raced to the rise, where he commanded a better view. The sound of hoofbeats carried over the dry, still air. A cloud of dust rose up behind the fleeing rider.

Morgan jacked another shell into the chamber.

Took aim, led Parsons a dozen feet. Squeezed. The rifle bucked against his shoulder. Captain Joe steadied himself. Orange flame scorched the air. A cloud of white smoke obscured Morgan's vision for a few moments. The smoke just hung there, then gradually broke up into gauzy wisps. The acrid smell of powder scratched at his nostrils.

Parsons topped a rise, then dipped out of sight, smacking leather.

Missed!

The range was long, though, and Morgan had no time to worry over the shot. It had put some ginger under Parsons's tail and rammed it high.

Captain Joe, though, didn't have another good chase in him just then. Morgan knew that. If he pushed him now, he might lose him. Forever. It would be better to rest him and grain him. Parsons would slow down soon. He couldn't hightail it for long. The man was a coward. A damned bushwhacker. When he knew Matling wasn't going to be in on it, he had run off instead of facing Morgan down. It was still another clue to the man's dubious character.

Parsons was headed south. Bypassing Benson, he could be in Tombstone by morning if he made a dry camp somewhere along the way. Morgan could press him, but it might be better to let him think he wasn't being chased. It was a good forty miles to Tombstone, but if Parsons thought he had eluded his pursuer, he might slow down. It was a hard forty-mile ride. Hard as hell.

He looked at the sun, marked its progress in the afternoon sky. He measured its distance from the western horizon by holding up his hand, counting the fingers between the sun and the earth. Six fingers. Fifteen minutes, approximately, to a finger. He had a good hour and a half before sunset. He might make another ten or fifteen miles, but that was doubtful. There was still the San Pedro to cross and rough country on both sides.

He sheathed the rifle after reloading it and let Captain Joe have his head. When he drifted, he brought him back on the track. Parsons was not hard to follow. He had broken some brush and left iron smears on

85

stones. The man was pushing his horse and there was a lot of heat left in the day.

There was a possibility that Parsons might have run out of food and water. If so, he might ride for one of the scattered ranches on the way to Benson. There was one big spread in particular that he would have to cross—the Jennings's. Pat Jennings was known far and wide for his hospitality to strangers. He didn't ask a lot of questions and he had plenty of spare bunk space. Pat's wife, Alice, made the best bear claws in the country. Their daughter, Lucinda, was a pretty fair cook, too. He would have sad news for them, but they had befriended him and Bonnie when they had first started setting up the ranch. It was the least he could do, stop by and ask if Parsons had been by, or Trask, and tell them what had happened. They would want to know. Captain Joe could have a few hours' rest, some hay and grain.

While the light held, Morgan followed Parsons's tracks. They continued to lead south, in the general direction of the Jennings spread northwest of Dragoon.

There was evidence that the man he was tracking had slowed down. He found a place where Parsons had alighted from his horse and relieved himself. In another spot, he found a burnt match and traces of tobacco. Here, horses' hooves had sunk deeper into the soft earth—a sure indication that Parsons had probably stopped to roll a quirly.

So, Parsons didn't know he was still being followed, or, if he did, he figured he was far enough ahead not to worry. Farther on, Parsons had left his horse to reconnoiter atop a jumble of rocks. So, the man was watching his backtrail every so often. The question was: did he know that Morgan was still behind him? Had he spotted Morgan from that vantage point?

There was no way to tell for sure. From the heat of the last horse droppings, Morgan figured that Parsons probably was at least an hour ahead. Maybe more. The steam had dissipated, but the droppings were still fairly warm. The heat of the day could account for some of the warmth.

A roadrunner startled Captain Joe as they tracked across a wide arroyo. Captain spooked and started hunting clouds, rearing back and sawing the air with his forefeet. Morgan hung on, cursing the roadrunner. He couldn't afford to fall off, risk injury. A man landing on hard earth could easily wrench his back out of place, or worse, break a leg or an arm. He steadied the animal, resolved to choke the horn a little tighter in the rough spots.

The miles flowed under Captain Joe's hooves as the sun dipped lower in the sky. Morgan stopped to water the animal and fill his own belly. The heat sapped him of strength, sucked out the fluids of his body through the pores of his skin.

The strain was beginning to tell. Bonnie and Tommy's deaths, the killing of Tío Pedro, and then the gun duel with Matling—all had tapped a hidden drainhole of energy. Fatigue weighted his muscles, began to fog his vision. He stretched, stood up in the stirrups. Rubbed his eyes. Yawned.

He began to see things that weren't there. Or if there, were not what he thought they were. Tall saguaros were men, standing bold, armed, ready to blow him out of the saddle. A rock moved, resembling a crawling figure. Sunlight danced on quartz and he thought a dozen rifles were aimed at him. Sometimes his ears strained at the silence and, at others, pounded from Captain Joe's hooves thudding into hard ground.

He rode right on by it, without noticing.

Cursing, Morgan wheeled Captain Joe, savagely jerking the reins. The bit cut into the horse's mouth cruelly.

But Parsons had circled.

He had almost missed it!

Damn!

Five minutes later, he picked up the track. It was true. Parsons had run out on him. He was no longer heading south, but had swung west. Now, Morgan was riding straight into the sun. He cursed himself for being a fool. He had let his mind wander and now he was at a disadvantage.

He pulled his hat brim low, but it did little good. If he dropped his head he wouldn't be able to see what lay ahead. If he kept it up . . . The sun clawed at his eyes with scorching molten fingers, blinding him to danger.

Parsons was no piker. He was plenty smart. His timing couldn't have been better.

The miles had lulled Morgan into a semistupor. The sun was low in the sky, almost level with his eyes.

Suddenly, Morgan realized that his quarry was no coward, but a dangerous man who played the odds. And now, the odds were in his favor.

Parsons, it seemed, had deliberately slowed down. The hour's distance had dwindled. To what? Minutes? Seconds?

The clam-cold moss of fear slithered into Morgan's belly. His eyes narrowed, flicked over the country ahead. The land was broken by arroyos, gullies, dry washes. Land ripped by waters cascading down from the mesas, the plateaus. A flash-flood land, where a sudden storm could sweep a man to his death in seconds, without warning. A land where concealment was easy. A land where death could wait and not be seen nor heard.

Morgan's scalp prickled as he slowly followed the new trail. It was painstaking work, made doubly hard by the need for caution. Parsons was being more careful now, too. The trail was more difficult to follow. Sometimes, Morgan had to dismount and search for a clue on foot: an overturned stone, a hoof mark in the dust, a bent or broken twig, the scar of a shoe on stone.

A prairie chicken drummed in the distance.

Morgan stopped, listened. A warning? His ears strained against the ensuing silence. He struggled to pinpoint the direction of the sounding.

A quail piped on a distant hill. *Cuh-cuh-cuh! Cuh-cuh-cuh!*

Morgan twisted in the saddle, sweeping the empty land with a searching gaze.

Silence again.

Long shadows stretched out over the land, stripping it with premonitions of dusk. Thin, high clouds battened the horizon with cottony rolls turning molten as the sun sank toward the far sea.

Morgan's nerves prickled with every sound now. A brace of prairie swifts sliced through the sky, veered off at right angles to a low hill ahead. A jackrabbit loped over the crest of a sage-dotted ridge, startled by something or someone a quarter mile off to the right.

Morgan's stomach knotted as the fear crawled in a

slow ooze through his groin. He dangled his right hand near the butt of his pistol, ready to snatch it from its leather at the first flicker of unnatural, unexpected movement.

The sun held on the horizon, a shimmering molten ball wreathed by fiery clouds. The top of its circle held aloft by jutting peaks.

Captain Joe gave him the first warning. The horse stopped, stiffened his ears and whinnied low.

Morgan clawed for his pistol. Metal whispered against leather.

An orange flower blossomed on a hill two hundred yards to the right. White smoke puffed into the air. The crack of the bullet racketed Morgan's ears a split second after the air sizzled inches from his head.

The skyline swallowed the sun, leaving golden-rimmed clouds framing the western sky like furled curtains waiting to fall on an empty stage.

A bullbat knifed past overhead, a tattered rag in the crepuscular silence that followed the shot.

He fired two futile shots from his pistol, reacting in anger and surprise. Muttering an incomplete oath, he rammed the pistol back in its leather and snatched at the butt of the Winchester.

Another shot cracked the stillness.

Morgan felt a hammering blow slam into his hip. He twisted in pain, the rifle half out of its sheath. A sticky wetness crawled down his right leg. Light-headed, he worked the rifle in what seemed to him slow motion. His hands moved like underwater birds as his vision swam with shimmering waves. A terrible weakness flooded through him. His arms turned leaden as the shock of the bullet drenched his senses. The clam-moss of fear hardened into a ball turning him sick. Bile rose up in his throat. He fought to stay himself from falling. The rifle came to his shoulder, and the darkening horizon blurred as the sky began to rust and purple. Wisps of smoke hung in the air, and he pulled the trigger again and again, with no effect.

The rifle wasn't cocked!

He brought it down, pushed against the lever. Slow! Too slow! The action was sluggish. He pushed on the lever and felt it give.

Captain Joe danced away in confusion, circled. Morgan swayed, lunged an arm out, a hand to grasp the horn.

Morgan gagged on the eruption in his throat.

The vomit surged up, strangling him. He sucked in particles. His air supply shut off as if someone had tripped a damper in his throat. The sky spun. The dusk churned to a smoky haze. Captain Joe whinnied as another shot fried the air, rang against the rocks, showering splintered projectiles of stone into the air. The rock slivers stung the horse's legs like primitive daggers. Captain Joe bolted and the rifle fell from Morgan's hands.

Another shot rang out.

He screamed as the bullet caught Morgan low in the back, ripping through the cantle.

Slowed down, the bullet twisted and tumbled as it slammed into him. A giant maul slammed into his flesh, pitching him forward over the saddle horn. Another bullet chilled his spine as it whistled between Captain Joe's ears.

The horse raced off at full speed, spurred by the showers of rock that stung his legs. In full gallop, Captain Joe flattened his ears. His tail streamed straight out from his hindquarters. His mane trailed backward, whipped by the wind of headlong flight.

Morgan held on, doubled up over the horn, waves of pain and nausea rolling through him, clouding his senses. Searing shots of purest agony rippled up his back and he didn't care. His hat blew off, and sprayed blood from his leg and back, stippled it before it fell.

There were no more shots.

Captain Joe took the bit in his teeth and raced as the darkness settled deep over the land. The horse got his second wind and raced on, southward, a dark wraith flying before the wind of his wake, flying like the wind itself, whipped on by fear and the odd feel of the lump on its back. His master wasn't in command. A dead weight rode his shoulders. The horse smelled blood and sweat and fear. His eyes rolled white in their sockets, his nostrils flared with exertion and strain.

Mile after mile, Captain Joe raced, then slowed.

The air changed.

The scent of water and grasses and cattle musked the air, weighted it with poignant aromas. A screech owl trilled. Bats sliced through the air, fangs bloodied from the rising sea of insects. A cow bawled.

Lights flickered just ahead.

But Morgan didn't see them. He didn't hear the challenge hurled into the night.

His left arm cradled the saddle horn in a death grip.

When the horse stopped, Morgan slid from the saddle. His body drummed heavily on the ground.

Voices swelled up about him.

A hand-held lantern swayed in the darkness, bathing him in a wobbly circle of light.

It lit the blood that drenched his hips and legs; lit the pale bone of his face so that it resembled a skull, a hideous death mask, waxen in the wavering glow of the lantern.

"It's Chad Morgan," Pat Jennings said. "And he's stone dead. Or damned near it."

A woman screamed.

Captain Joe whickered quietly, casting a gimlet eye on his fallen master.

CHAPTER TEN

Luke Trask snapped the frayed matchstick in half with his teeth. "Fred, you ain't got the sense God gave a coon! You peckerwood! I didn't tell you to set fire to Morgan's place."

"Hell, I thought you'd be mighty proud we burned him out."

"Yair? Well, where in hell's Harley?"

"I told you. I don't know." Parsons sat at the back table in the Lone Wolf, wondering when Trask was going to offer him a drink of whiskey. The bottle sat between them. The barkeep had brought the extra glass over at least five minutes ago. It was midmorning and Parsons had ridden all night from Dragoon. Breakfast had been put away three hours before. It had taken him a good two hours to find Trask. He had looked for him at the Occidental and at the Orient, but here he was holed up in a second-rate saloon with rooms in back and upstairs.

"Don't know, or don't want to know?" Trask sneered.

"Hell, he might have made it. I just saw his horse, that's all. And his horse didn't make it."

"Harley was a pretty good man."

Trask spat out splinters of wood, searched through his vest for a fresh matchstick. He was still bleary-eyed from a night out on the town. Tombstone was wide open, split into factions of hardcases. As long as a man kept to his own bunch, he was all right. It was when he tried to get in good with one or another of the other bunches that he was liable to be back-shot. Curly Bill Brocius and his men were holding their own with Wyatt Earp and his faction, but the tension in town was like a wet strip of rawhide drying in the sun. Ever since the Clantons and the Earps and Doc Holliday had shot it out at the O.K. Corral, nobody trusted anybody else in Tombstone.

"Harley was right enough," Parsons ventured, licking his dry lips.

"That's all? What about Chad Morgan? You see him after that?"

"He's likely dead, Trask. You gonna share that whiskey?"

Trask snapped his head back as if cuffed by a bear. "What?" he roared. "Morgan dead?"

"Maybe. I shot him. Shot him bad."

Trask's eyes narrowed to feral slits. "You sonofabitch," he breathed. "He was mine. Mine!"

"Dammit, Trask, just listen, will you? The man was pressing me hard. He probably blowed Harley out of the saddle and then come after me. I was just defending myself. Got him good, too." A flicker of a smile played on the corners of Fred's mouth.

"You better tell me all of it, Fred."

Trask shoved the bottle angrily across the table. Parsons picked it up on the fly and ran a healthy stream of whiskey down the spout and into his glass. He took the bite and his eyes watered. He held on until the nausea settled and the warmth spread through his gut. The barkeep at the rough-board bar eyed him as he trimmed the bottles on the back bar.

"Ah," Fred breathed, with a shudder of pleasure. "That takes the kinks out of the backbone. I been ridin' hard all night."

"Get to Morgan."

"The man's a tracker. Horse all tuckered out and he stuck to me like furniture glue. So, I figured I'd circle him and get the drop on him. He'd have the sun square in his eyes and then it would be dark in case I didn't make it. I had him cold, Trask. First shot hit him in the leg. Any other man would have howled and gone flying out of the saddle. Morgan stuck. I blasted him fast as I could shoot, hit him again. I don't know . . . the back, the lung."

"And so he dropped?"

Fred shook his head, toyed with his glass. "Hell, he took off. That big horse of his fair went flying. It was dark as the inside of a coal mine by then, but I took off after him. Found his hat. Blood all over it. Blood trail for a long ways."

"So, where is he?"

"Dead, I reckon. I backtracked, saw all the blood. Like a gut-shot deer. Hell, he wouldn't have made five miles. I figger he's bein' picked over by turkey buzzards right about now."

Trask looked unconvinced. He stroked his beard, chewed on the matchstick.

"You sure that's what happened, Fred? I don't want no surprises. I got things set up here now and I'd hate like hell for them to get spoiled."

"I swear," Fred said. He tossed back the last of his drink, wiped his damp lips with his sleeve.

Trask poured him another drink. Drank a finger of his own. He was pacing himself, but now he felt he could relax. A man hit that bad wouldn't come walking in unexpected. Morgan was either dead or so bad wounded he would be stove up for a long time. Or, he might die sometime soon. Trask cracked a forgiving smile.

"Hell, you did good, Fred. Saved me the trouble. I just wisht you'd brought me back a piece of his hide, that's all."

"I got his hat out in my saddlebags. Bloody as a monthly rag."

Trask grinned. He motioned to Nuñez, who had finished the bar and was sneaking a bean-filled tortilla into his mouth. He slipped the morsel back under the counter and shuffled over to the table.

"The one was here, yesterday," Trask said. "Curly. Fetch him. Not Brocius, but the *pelon*. You savvy?"

"*Sí*. Curlee. He aslip now. No hair. *Pelado*. I get him for you, Señor Trask."

"Curly?" asked Fred. "Curly Bill?"

"No, this is another Curly. This one don't have hair like Bill Brocius. He's pure bald. Bald as a cue ball."

Fred screwed up his face. Shook his head. "Don't know him."

"Jack Curly Garth. He might work out. Now that Harley's gone and Higgins is under cover, we need another man."

Quickly, Trask briefed Parsons on what Higgins had done. He didn't tell him that Curly Garth was no more than a footpad who would sell out his employer, if not his best friend. He wasn't in the habit of telling his confederates all that he did and, in this case, he was not proud. It was just as bad to pay a man for betraying a friend as it was to actually betray one. Yet he had no conscience about what he had done. Morgan had got what he deserved. In fact, he had lived too long with a woman who hadn't belonged to him.

Trask had another drink of the good whiskey. Parsons filled his own glass without asking.

Curly Garth appeared, disheveled, carrying his boots in his hand. He sat down, slipped them on while Nuñez went back to his clandestine tortilla.

"Curly, this here's Fred Parsons. Shake hands, boys, and then let's take a walk. Walls have ears."

"What's up?" Curly asked.

"We'll see," Trask said, lurching to his feet. He wasn't drunk. He had an enormous capacity for alcohol. It was a thing he had once been proud to boast, but now he wondered if it wasn't a curse. It took more and more to put him away and he felt worse for a longer time afterward. But good whiskey was hard to come by and he couldn't pass up Old Overholt after months of tanglefoot or Taos Lightning.

"Put the bottle back, Nuñez. Be back later," Trask called to the Mexican barkeep.

The bright sun painted the false fronts yellowish-green, the dust-clogged streets a pale lemon. Thin clouds hazed the light, softened the adobes. Trask turned up Fourth Street, away from the clatter of merchants. A skeletal cur, its shaggy tail curled under its hindquarters, dodged the trio as they took to the center of the street.

"Curly," Trask said. "You still want to join my outfit?"

"I sure as heck do, Trask."

"You got to follow orders. No questions."

"I'm your man. I been thinkin' about this a long time."

Parsons said nothing.

Trask stopped at the corner, looked around. He tossed away the soaked and shredded matchstick in his mouth and looked at the two men.

"Parsons here thinks he put Morgan down. He 'dobe-walled him up in the Dragoons and it might be that we won't be troubled anymore. Still, I took out some insurance. Yesterday. Now I got to add to it. Now I can't use Parsons here. Somebody might remember him and me being together. So, it falls on you, Curly. That man in the sheriff's office, you met yesterday, working under Rushmore, he's one part of the insurance policy."

Parsons's eyebrows went up.

"Delbert Harris," Trask said.

Parsons nodded. He knew Trask meant Dave Higgins. Harris was an alias Dave had used from time to time when dodging the law.

"And the second part?" Garth asked, sliding his hat off his head and running fingers over his smooth pate.

Parsons's jaw dropped when he saw the gleaming head.

"Watch you don't get sunburnt," he cracked wryly.

"He's heard it all before, Fred. Listen." Trask pierced Parsons with a look. "Curly, I want you to report to that deputy and tell him you heard Chad Morgan say he was going to kill his wife and kid and set fire to his place."

"That's all?" Curly asked.

"That's all. Be right sure about it, too. You heard him tell you that when you left Fort Huachuca."

"Why?" Curly asked.

" 'Cause Sheriff Rushmore will take that real serious if you do a good job of acting and he'll send someone up to check on it."

Curly whistled in admiration.

Parsons, too, looked at Trask with a new respect.

"Then if Morgan shows up in Tombstone, he'll get run into the hoosegow faster'n you can say Peckerwood Holler," Parsons said. "I got to hand it to you, Luke Trask, you don't leave no rope ends dangling."

Trask cracked a smile.

A pair of women in long dresses passed by, their faces shaded by sunbonnets. They carried woven baskets filled with cloth goods purchased on Allen Street from a cut-rate drummer. The men were silent until they passed. But it was time to move on. Too many people were noticing their small huddle at the corner.

The three men turned the corner of Allen, crossed the wide street that even now was lined with horses, mules, wagons. A hurdy-gurdy wheezed mournfully down the street. Snatches of laughter floated from inside one of the bawdier cantinas. This was a street of life, tucked back out of sight, gaudy, raucous, untamed. Saloons and whorehouses dominated the trade. This was where the cheaper rooming houses catered to men on their way up or on their way down.

Rudy Owens stared at the trio as they crossed the street.

Their backs were to him as he sat in the shade on the porch of the New Mexico: Rooms—50 cents and Up.

He recognized Curly Garth. The big-bearded man—he had seen him before . . . in the Lone Wolf. He knew his name, too. Luke Trask. The other man he did not know. But now he knew why Curly didn't want him around anymore. If he was hooking up with Trask, he was getting his wish: to ride with the wild bunch. Any wild bunch. Brocius and Ringo had turned him down. The Earps wouldn't give him the time of day. But there he was with Trask and he looked as if he was one of the bunch already.

Rudy made note of what he saw. Information was information. It might not mean much now, but it might sometime in the future.

The men passed out of earshot, and Rudy dug in his vest for makings. He rolled a fat quirly, found a match, lit it. The smoke bit into his throat, clawed his lungs. He leaned the chair back against the wall of the decrepit hotel. Maybe he wouldn't look for work just yet. He would give it another day or two. See what happened.

Trask stopped outside a Mexican cantina. It was noisy inside. None of the Mexicans paid any attention to them. That suited Trask just fine.

"I got a job lined up for us," Trask said, his voice just barely above a whisper. "Listen close."

Curly and Fred crowded close to Trask.

A guitar struck up a plaintive series of chords. Someone in the cantina began singing a sad *son huasteco*, full of tears and heartache, a song of love and betrayal and death. Trask ignored it and raised his voice slightly.

"It's pretty quiet right now," he said. "There's bad blood between Brocius and the Earps. Wyatt got himself appointed marshal and he's off chasing Curly Bill somewhere down around Bisbee or over to Nogales. There hasn't been a stage robbery in weeks."

"So?" Curly Garth asked. "You gonna rob a stage?"

Parsons grinned.

"You don't know how we work, do you, Baldy?"

Curly shook his head.

"Trask mocks what these other jaspers do," Parsons said. "He's a reg'lar damned mockin'bird, that's what!"

"Shut up, Fred," Trask said.

"Hell, Trask, he's one of us, ain't he?"

"You tell him all this bullshit later. Now we got business."

Trask outlined the plan quickly. It was simple. Curly's eyes brightened like brass buttons.

"We hit the stage in ten days just outside of Pantano. You get yourself a wig, Curly, and the biggest bandanna you can find. Get a real hairy, curly one. You're gonna be Curly Bill Brocius. We'll have Wyatt Earp in fits. Fred and I'll pack the Greeners, you just be sure you throw down on the shotgunner until we brace them. We won't talk during the robbery, so you got to get it straight before we jerk that stage to a halt."

"You mean we're . . . I'm supposed to be Curly Bill?" Garth asked.

"You do hear good, don't you?" Trask asked.

Parsons dug an elbow in Curly's side.

Winked.

"What'd I tell you? Everybody'll be blaming Curly Bill for this one. Earp's looking for him down South, and we make him think the hairy bastard is up North. It's perfect. Trask, you got a set of brains."

"Fuck you, Parsons," Trask said. But he was pleased. He had himself a new bunch. It was time to ride.

CHAPTER ELEVEN

The voices drifted in and out of his mind like bubbles from a child's pipe. The words were all watery and fluid, almost formless. He couldn't make any sense of them. At times they sounded logical, and at others they might as well have been in a foreign language.

He heard his name every so often and wondered if he was dead. He didn't know if he was awake or not, but thought he might be deep asleep. He couldn't see anything and didn't want to see anything. He thought that if he opened his eyes he would just see a red haze or pitch darkness.

Where was he?

Something cool touched his forehead. Cool and damp.

A voice murmured something soft in his ear.

From far off he felt the heat. A heat that turned to pain when he thought about it. Every time he thought he would open his eyes and get up, he felt himself sinking back down . . . down into a place where there was no air and no words and no sound. A place of quiet pain that was not his pain—just pain . . . existing . . . next to him. It was close enough to touch if he were capable of touching. He seemed to be floating on the pain at times. At others, he was sure he must be bathing in it. But now, it was just there, somewhere out of reach, throbbing, pulsing, waiting.

The sounds drifted away and he heard only a blood-red silence.

The pain rose up to him then, drenching him, sucking away his breath. He felt his mouth opening. He heard himself scream, but there was no sensation of screaming. The sound, like the pain, was his, but somehow disconnected—as if he had two bodies, as if he were one of a set of twins.

The voices came back, like the sounds of animals . . . or birds—chattering, humming, growling.

His ears buzzed and rang.

"Chad! Chad!"

His name! That was his name.

"Bonnie!" he screamed.

"Oh, my goodness. He's still delirious. Lucinda, bring the soup!"

"Yes, Mother."

Morgan's eyes opened feebly. The room swam around him. Pain sawed at his brain. Sawed through bone. A streak of fire raced up his leg. A chunk of molten metal burned into his hip.

"Jesus," he muttered.

"Pat! Come quick!" Alice Jennings yelled, leaning over the bed.

Morgan saw a comely woman in her late thirties, hair bundled up on her head streaked with gray, soft blue eyes, a strong chin and straight nose that hooked slightly at the end. She wore a pinafore over a simple cotton dress. He felt a hand on his arm.

"Chad," she whispered, "thank God you're awake. Pat will be here in a moment."

"Alice?"

"Yes. You're alive! Lucinda is bringing some broth. Oh, you impossible man, you! You scared us half to death." She squeezed his arm.

Chad was surprised that he could feel her touch. And the pain. He tried to turn his head, but the pain brought him up short. He felt the bandages tight around his chest . . . bandages on his back and hips. The room smelled of carbolic acid and liniment and perfume. It had the scrubbed smell of fresh milk on Sunday mornings.

"How'd I get here?" he asked, his mouth full of cotton. His hearing was still off. Alice sounded as if she were talking underwater. The ringing in his ears was loud, as if someone had struck a churchbell with a sledge. The single note was steady.

"Don't try to talk. Just listen. Oh, wait a minute, here's Pat."

A tall, slender man with a mustache and sideburns loomed over the edge of the bed. His thin brown hair was slicked back. His shoulders were wide and he stretched out a hand that was small, brown as a gnarled oak knot and just as hard. Morgan managed to raise a hand to take Pat's. He felt the squeeze and was again surprised that he had normal feeling.

"Chad, son, you're in a bad way. But we're fixing you up. I sent Hector up to your place to fetch Bonnie, Tommy, and Tío Pedro. Lucinda can watch little Tommy while your woman nurses you back to health."

"See, Chad," Alice said brightly, "there's not a thing to worry about. Hector will be here tonight or in the morning with Bonnie, little Tommy, and Tío Pedro."

"No," Morgan croaked. Pain thundered through his body. He closed his eyes. Closed them like doubled-up fists. "No! Dammit, no!"

Alice shrank away from the bed.

Pat scowled. "Now listen, son," he said. "We're only trying to do what's best. You've been out cold for two days and Hector couldn't go until this morning. Hell, it's taken everyone here a whole lot of time just to keep you breathing. You must've lost ten gallons of blood and I had to cut out a piece of bullet big as your little fingernail that was workin' its way to a mighty big vessel in your leg. There ain't a sawbones within twenty mile of here."

Lucinda entered the room at that moment.

She was a petite young woman of eighteen, with her mother's pale blue eyes, her father's dark hair. Her pert, upturned nose gave her the look of a pixie, and when she smiled, deep dimples etched themselves into the corners of her mouth. She was firm-breasted, trim, with a supple, hour-glass figure that refused to stay concealed under the crinoline frock she wore. She carried a tray laden with a steaming cup of broth, a large spoon, and a cast iron pot with the lid on it.

Pat stepped aside to let his daughter pass. Alice drifted to the foot of the bed.

"Hello, Chad," Lucinda said. "It's good to see you awake. Have some broth." She set the tray down on the table next to the bed and picked up the cup. Morgan stared at her, dazed.

"I know you can't sit up," Lucinda told him, "so

107

I'll have to hold your head up like I been doin' these past two days. I won't have to feed you with the spoon. You can drink from the cup."

"Huh?" Morgan said. "I've been here two days?"

"Three is more like it," Pat said. "And a night. A hellish night."

"You talk, Pa. Chad, you hush and let me feed you this hot broth. You need your strength."

Helplessly, Morgan lay there as Lucinda expertly slung an arm around his neck and forced his head up. She put the cup up to his lips, tilted it. Beef, chunks of potatoes, leeks, hot broth, poured into his mouth, down his throat.

Morgan allowed Lucinda to feed him the broth. He could almost feel its strength flooding him. His hunger was acute and he chewed the beef greedily.

"Good!" Lucinda exclaimed with relief. "We were really worried about you."

Morgan lay back, sated. He had put away two mugs of broth.

"Pat," he said weakly. "let me talk to you alone."

Pat looked at his wife and daughter.

"Of course," Alice said. "Come on, Lucinda, we've things to do."

"Thanks," Morgan said. "Both of you. I'm deeply grateful."

"It's our pleasure," Alice said. "You'll feel better when Bonnie gets here to take care of you."

Morgan winced.

Pat waited until the door closed, then drew up a chair and sat by the bed. His weather-tanned face was heavily veined. He had spent most of his life outdoors and the wind and sun had etched hard lines next to his nose, around his mouth, in his forehead. He looked at Morgan with concern, the crow's-feet next to his eyes crinkling into deep furrows.

"What's on your mind, Chad?"

"Hector's not going to find Bonnie, Pat. Or Tommy. Or Tío Pedro. Only their graves. They're all dead."

"Dead? Are you still out of your head, son?"

Morgan grimaced, then haltingly he told Jennings what had happened. He left out nothing except his own shock and grief. He told him of Ned Trask and Luke, of the burning of the house, the tracking of the two men. Matling and Parsons.

"Parsons suckered me good. I walked right into it."

Pat Jennings drew a breath. He shook his head sadly; put a hand on Morgan's, squeezed it manfully. "I'm damned sorry, Chad," he said quietly.

"I'd be obliged if you'd tell the womenfolk."

"Yeah."

"How bad am I bunged up, Pat?"

"Could be worse. You lost a lot of blood. I took that chunk of lead out, but it was only a splinter. Nothing cut that won't heal. You just gotta take it slow and easy for a time."

"I'm going after Trask, Pat. And Parsons. Higgins, too. I've got a special boil for that bastard. He's the one that roped Tommy, dragged him."

"Jesus, Chad. You ain't going nowheres for a time. Matter of fact, me and Alice were fixin' to go to Tucson when you came in all bloodied up. We got business there that just won't wait. Be gone a week or two, but you can stay here. Lucinda can take care of you."

Morgan tried to rise. A sickening pain wrenched him back in place.

"Don't try it, Chad," Jennings warned. "You lost about a gallon of red juice and it's going to take a lot of beef to get you back on your feet."

Morgan nodded. His eyes were heavy. It was no use trying to do something he couldn't. Pat was right. He needed to build himself back up. Trask and the others could wait. If they weren't in Tombstone, they'd be somewhere else. He would find them. Even if he had to ride to the ends of the earth. He'd find the bastards!

"When you leaving, Pat?"

"We were going to wait until . . . that is, until Hector got back. But we ought to leave right away. Today. It's real important."

"You go on. I'll be okay. Week or two will see me through this. I guess nothing broke."

Pat shook his head. "You got two clean holes in you. Lucinda knows how to pack 'em, change the bandages. She'll be your nurse. She did it all anyway. She does the same for a horse, any of the beeves. Reg'lar little doctorer, she is."

"I owe you much, Pat. You go on to Tucson. Reckon I'll be here when you get back. My horse . . ."

"Captain Joe's fine. Lucinda took him under her wing, too. Runs him with the whip purt near ever' day and spoilin' him with grain. He brought you here and I reckon we're mighty grateful for that."

Morgan closed his eyes.

Pain washed over him. But already he felt stronger. He was alive. He would heal.

"You get some sleep, son," Pat said. "If I don't see you before we leave, *adiós*."

"*Vaya* . . ." Morgan breathed. His eyes fluttered.

He sank back down into somnolence, let the broth do its work. He was asleep before Pat closed the door.

He awoke in darkness. His mouth was dry. A rumbling pain throbbed in his hip, answered by a throb in his lower back. His tongue flicked over dessicated lips.

"Water!" he whispered to himself.

His eyes adjusted to the gloom. A crack of light seeped under the door. He reached for the glass at his bedside. The pain scorched him from thigh to brain. His fingers closed around the glass.

It fell just as the door opened. The glass hit the floor with a splintering crash as light flooded the room.

Lucinda, in a nightgown, stood in the doorway, a lamp in her hand.

"Chad!"

The light bobbled toward him as he sank back on the bed.

"Water!" he said again. "I'm bone-dry, Lucinda."

She set the lamp on the bedside table. Her slippers crunched on the broken glass.

"Oh, dear. I'll bring you another glass."

"The pitcher. Just give me the pitcher."

She held the pitcher to his lips. Water slopped into his throat. He choked, cleared his air passage, and drew the water into his mouth in hungry gulps. Lucinda kept pouring. Morgan kept drinking. His mouth and throat were parched. The water soothed the arid membranes, softened the parchment-hard tissues. He drank the whole pitcher, lay back exhausted.

She placed a hand on his forehead. "You've got the fever again."

111

Morgan began to shake with chill. "I . . . I'm freezing," he said.

"The water does that, I guess." She stood up, pulled another comforter up over him. Morgan continued to shiver. His teeth chattered like dice in a box.

"Lucinda," he said. "I think one of my wounds broke open. I feel wet."

"Did you use the bedpan?" she chided.

"Jesus, Lucinda."

"Don't swear." She smiled at him warmly. "I'll have to turn you over. It's probably that back wound. The one Pa took a sliver of lead out of. He had to cut it some. I sewed you up, but you might have slipped a stitch."

"You sewed me up?"

"Just like a rag doll."

He looked at her helplessly. The woman had worked on him and he didn't know anything about it. It was just as well. He had no clothes on. She would have had to see him that way. It was probably she who emptied the slop bucket, too—what she called a bedpan. It was pure hell trying to use the damned thing.

Lucinda gently turned him over on his stomach. She did it so deftly, he thought she must have trained to be a nurse, but he knew that wasn't so. She was just like a hundred other women in the territory. They learned how to make do with what they had. What they had was a lot of uncommon common sense.

He felt the bandage come off. A slight tearing sound, pressure on his flesh.

"You've got a little ooze. Infected, probably. That's why you have the fever."

"Dammit, I'm cold!"

"Hush now, swear-mouth. I'm going to put some healing herbs on there and then I'll see to it that you're warm."

"Hell, I'm smothering under blankets."

"There are other ways to keep you warm," she said softly.

CHAPTER TWELVE

Chad Morgan's fever raged, off and on, for a week. Lucinda hovered over him constantly, like a ministering angel. He was only dimly aware of her. Once, he thought he had touched a bare breast. Another time, he felt a bare leg against his. It was difficult to separate dream from reality.

Once, Hector came in to see him, weeping and wringing his battered hat in his hands. He spoke wildly in Spanish, expressing sympathies over Morgan's wife and son, bewailing the fact that Tío Pedro—beloved Tío Pedro Gomez—had been killed, and his daughter on her way here from Sonora. Poor Gabriela Gomez, orphaned now, out of the convent and expecting to embrace her father. What would she do now, all alone and her only relative buried under a heap of stones in the devil's own country? Lucinda had shooed Hector away, protecting Morgan from visitors.

She moved in and out of his room like an angel so that he wondered, at times, if he was alive or dead and possibly in heaven.

He knew that she had kept him warm with her own body heat. It was something he did not want to talk about just yet. It staggered him that she could do that for him. When he was awake, he was embarrassed to know this thing. He avoided looking at her directly, but only gazed at her when she was busy doing something else and did not look him in the eye.

When the fever broke, he knew he was finally on the mend.

Lucinda came in with a breakfast tray. Morgan sat up. There was no pain, only a couple of tugs where the wounds were.

"My but you look human this morning," she said gaily. "Or you will after I shave you."

He felt his face. A thick growth of beard scratched his fingers. "Ouch," he laughed.

She set the tray on his lap, touched his forehead. He looked her in the eyes. Close. There was something there. A light. Compassion. Tenderness. His heart sank. Lucinda was beautiful. He wondered if he had fallen in love with her so soon after losing Bonnie. No, it was just a curiosity. He had heard stories from men who had fought in the war about falling in love with their nurses. Some of the nurses were hags, but that didn't make any difference.

Lucinda returned his gaze, strong for a moment, full of meaning. Then, she dropped her eyes shyly.

"Thank you, Lucinda," he said. "I'm mighty glad you pulled me through."

"Oh, pshaw, you're strong. I noticed you didn't use the bedpan last night."

"I got up, went outside."

"Did it hurt?"

"Not much. My muscles are all kinked up, though."

"You'll be sore and tender for a while. Now, eat your breakfast while I boil some water. I'm going to shave you, whether you like it or not. You scratch."

They both blushed.

Morgan looked down at the tray. There were eggs, biscuits, bacon, beans, a thin strip of beefsteak, a steaming cup of black coffee. He attacked the breakfast voraciously as Lucinda tripped out of the room, returning a few minutes later with a bowl of steaming water.

The solid food was the first he'd had in ten days. He drank three cups of coffee before Lucinda accused him of stalling so that he wouldn't have to get a shave.

"Not true," he said. "But I can shave myself."

"You can, but I'm used to it. You have a nice soft face."

"You chide me, Lucinda."

"Well, you've been a pretty sick boy. There was no need for you to look like a grizzly bear, was there? I enjoyed shaving you."

"I can't thank you enough."

She brought the hot water, lathering soap, a brush, mug, and straight razor. Morgan admired her dexterity. The truth was, he didn't know if he could have managed to shave himself. Lying down, maybe, but his legs were still weak. He enjoyed the touch of Lucinda's hands. Bonnie wouldn't mind, he knew. Or would she?

He had to stop thinking that way. Bonnie was gone. Somehow, he was alive. There were men he had to see. That was the only reason for his existence now. Later, perhaps, he could piece together what had happened, come to some agreement with himself. Bonnie was still

116

strong in his memory, but he couldn't let her weigh him down. Lucinda was a good woman, no more than a girl, really, and she had become mighty important. If it wasn't for her taking care of him, he probably wouldn't have made it.

"When're your folks coming back?" he asked, as she was rubbing his face clean of lather.

"Hector brought a letter from them yesterday. Came to Benson. They'll be back soon."

"Soon?"

"A few days. A week. I wish they'd take another month, don't you?"

He looked into her cobalt eyes, trying to fathom if there was any meaning beyond her words. The smoky depths told him nothing, but there was the faintest curl to her lips as if she was cautioned not to reveal a hidden secret.

"It's a long time," he faltered. "A month."

"You need a month of peace and quiet."

She was right, he knew. It would be at least a month before he could sit his saddle without tearing something loose. Still, a month with Lucinda could be like a year in an Apache war camp. She was a young, desirable woman and he was a widower. It was like mixing fire and coal oil. He vowed to give her no reason to test his willpower, his resolve to keep to his own side of the fence. He hoped Pat and Alice Jennings would be back soon.

"I'd like to take a bath sometime this morning," he said, "and get some clothes on. Maybe I could sit outside in the sun this afternoon."

"I gave you a bath every day, Mister Morgan."

"You did?" His jaw dropped a good inch.

"Such as it was."

"You have me at the cornerpost," he said. "I didn't know."

"Well, there's a lot of you to wet and lather, Chad."

He changed the subject as he felt the heat rise up his neck, tingle his face.

"What's your father doin' down in Tucson, anyways?"

"He sold three hundred horses and he wants to invest some of the money. He was to meet a man in Tucson."

Morgan whistled. "Pat's got a head on his shoulders. He's done right well. Not like me and my three-up outfit."

"Don't talk that way, Chad. Pa said you did just fine after starting out with not enough beef to hold a barbecue. He and Ma started out worse'n you did and it took them longer to get out of the well hole."

"Breakin' horses is a lot harder than growin' beeves."

"Except in this country, where grass is scarcer'n hen's teeth."

Morgan laughed. Lucinda had a sense of humor. She could give tit for tat. He threw up his arms in mock surrender. "What's this about Tío Pedro's daughter Hector was babbling about? Did I dream that?"

"No, it's true, I'm afraid." Lucinda cleared away the shaving paraphernalia, stacking it with the dishes on the tray. She brushed crumbs from his bed, pushed back a stray hair dangling next to her ear. "Gabriela Gomez is due to arrive in Nogales day after tomorrow. Hector's going to fetch her. I imagine we'll take her in, if she wants to stay."

118

"Pedro set great store by her. Talked of that girl a heap."

"He thought a lot of you, too, Chad. And he loved little Tommy."

"I know. I miss them terrible, Lucinda. I guess I always will."

"I'm sorry. I shouldn't have—"

"No. I can't keep burying it. It happened. You can't pussyfoot around me. It would make me damned nervous."

Lucinda swooped up the tray and started for the door. "You know, Chad," she said, "you curse too damned much!"

They both laughed, and Morgan was still chuckling after she had gone. The pain seemed to go away when she was around.

It was a bad sign.

Or a good one.

Chad lay on the bed, hands folded behind his head, his arms winged on the pillow. He listened to the night sounds—crickets tuning up like a scattered orchestra of sawyers, a coyote yapping on a ridge, a horse nickering for reassurance in the corral.

The guest room, where he was staying, was sparsely furnished, but Lucinda had spruced it up with bright flowers Hector had given her. He had not noticed the room at all until the past couple of days. A religious picture hung on one wall, a Currier & Ives in a cheap frame on another. Deep windows with outside shutters were sunk into the adobe, a gun port was cut in the wood. A bedside table, a highboy dresser, another table and a pair of high-backed chairs streaked with the remnants of the original varnish, and a wardrobe in one corner, where his patched clothes and pistol hung completed the furnishings. He would have to buy clothes and a new rifle.

The wounds were healing fast. Herbs and the salt baths had crimped the stitched flesh, closed off the leaks. The wounds itched now and had changed color. The infection was gone. Sun and good food had furthered the healing process. Exercise—careful exercise—had strengthened the melding flesh underneath the stitches. There was a little pain, just a twinge now and then, a tug at a sore spot if he moved too fast or tried to bend over. He was putting on weight, but that was all right. He had lost some pounds during the fever time.

Lucinda had been good to him—good *for* him—never crowding him, letting him go at his own pace, treating him like a babe trying to learn how to walk. She never mentioned the nights she had lain with him, heating his body with hers as he rattled with chill. Nor had he said anything. But it was between them. And, sometimes, when he looked at her from a distance, he thought she was Bonnie. Hoped that it had all been a dream and Bonnie was alive, bustling about the house, fixing his meals, preparing his bed.

He could not sleep now, thinking of her. Not Bonnie. Lucinda.

It had gotten worse after Hector had left that morning knowing they were alone together. All alone. The tension had been there, although neither had acknowledged it. His loins swarmed with heat now, thinking of her. Thinking of those times when her naked body had

120

warmed him and he'd been too sick to care. Between deliriums, thinking of her warm touches.

A chorus of coyotes began yapping, bright ribbons of animal laughter floating on the clear night air. Maybe they were chasing deer or rabbits. Playing. A female in heat, perhaps. Captain Joe whinnied. Chad was like a man whistling in the dark, hoping nothing would happen, but secretly sure that something *would* happen. In the dark, each shadow was a danger, a threat. In the dark, a man's thoughts were sometimes crazy.

He wished the lamp were lit. He wished he were a hundred miles away—away from temptation.

Moonlight limned the windowsill, seeped into the room, shrouding it with pewter dust.

The house stirred with movement.

Lamp glow wavered down the hall, came toward him. He pulled the sheet over his nakedness. Just a sheet? What the hell was he trying to do? You could see through the damned thing, for Chrissakes!

"Chad? You awake?"

"Huh? Yeah, I guess so."

"Me, too. I can't sleep."

Lucinda floated into the room, a pale nightgown clinging to her naked body. The cloth rustled against her bare legs. Her face glowed copper-orange behind the lamp's glass chimney. Her features were softened by the shadows, her eyes brilliant glitters, sparkling with light.

"It's so quiet. The horses are jumpy," she said. She set the lamp next to the bed, sat on the edge.

She was close. Close enough to touch. Spirals of soft hair coiled down from her temples, framed her delicate face. He smelled her musk, scarcely hidden by the faint perfume she wore.

He propped himself up with an elbow, rolled over on his side, looked at her in the lampglow. Moonlight caught in her hair, a silver tangle in the fine wisps. He didn't say anything. He didn't trust himself to say a word just then.

"Hector will be back tomorrow," she said. "With Gabriela Gomez."

"Yes."

"Pa and Ma could come anytime. Not tonight, though. Tomorrow. Next day." Her voice was edged with sadness.

"Lucinda," he murmured, "it's not right, you know. For either of us."

"What?" Her eyes widened in surprise. "Oh! Oh, Chad! Don't say that. Not now."

"I have to say it."

"No!" She turned, fell on his chest. Her hair tumbled over his shoulders. The sheet slipped down from her weight. She put her arms around him, held him. She was trembling.

"Lucinda . . ."

"Oh, God, I know it's wrong. It's too soon. I'm horrible. But I want you, Chad Morgan. More than anything in the world, I want you. Please, don't send me away. I couldn't bear it. I couldn't!"

"Neither could I," he whispered in her ear as he drew her closer.

CHAPTER THIRTEEN

The Overland Stage lumbered out of Pantano, furls of dust streaming in twin spirals behind the boot. Six horses strained at their harness straps as the driver yelled and cracked a thin whip over their heads. The stage was running an hour late and Alf Swensen, the driver, worked his team as if they were mules. The shotgun man, Neil Yates, hung on to the rail, dug in his boot heels as the coach swayed, gaining momentum.

Inside the Concord, Pat Jennings savored the aroma of a cheroot, carefully blowing the smoke out the window. Alice fanned herself with a paper fan bought in Tucson, moving the hot air against her face to give her the sensation of coolness.

The other passenger, a drummer from St. Louis who had ridden all the way from Ramona in California, was a florid-faced man in his late thirties who had spent too much time with John Barleycorn. Spiderwebs—thin red lines—laced his face. His cheeks were purpling, the pores oversize to the point of almost being pocks. He sipped from a bottle of medicant that fooled no one.

The fumes from his breath reeked inside the careening coach.

"Well, we're getting closer to home," Alice said. "I can't wait to see Lucinda's face when I show her all the pretties I bought her."

"I just hope she can handle the situation there," Pat said, expelling a plume of smoke out the window. The smoke was snatched by the wind and swallowed up by the rooster tails of dust spooling out of the Concord's wheeltracks.

"You mean Chad Morgan?"

"I do. He's a handful. Taking care of a wounded man can be choresome."

"Are you talking about me, Pat Jennings?" Alice squeezed his arm teasingly. "The time you were all stove up from being caught afoot by that old mossyhorn. Why, you were a baby, until you started getting better. Then you were ornery. Downright ornery."

"I'm talking about that time. And others. Man not used to being bedridden gets mighty touchy at being waited on hand and foot."

"You loved it," she chided.

"For about ten minutes. Chad will want to be up and about and Lucinda will try and keep him down. We stayed away too damned long."

"Hector's there. He'll keep an eye on things. If Lucinda needs help, Hector can give it to her."

"Yair. Guess so."

The drummer looked at the two seated across from him. His rheumic eyes tried to focus in the swaying compartment.

"Someone sick at home?" Homer Morrison asked. "Happens I drum a line of medical products that are

124

the finest in the land, bar none. And not just one brand, either. Nor any homemade snake-bite remedies. No, sirree, sir, you bet your bottom dollar, Homer Morrison sells only the best. What ails the child?"

"Bullet wounds," Pat growled. "Lead poisoning. You got any cure for that?"

Morrison seemed to shrink in his seat as Jennings withered him with a stern look.

"Sorry," the drummer said. "Just trying to help. The name's Homer Morrison. I hail from Ellsworth, in Kansas Territory. Work out of St. Louis."

Pat blew a plume of smoke straight at Morrison. Alice kicked his boot, shot him a disapproving glance.

Morrison hacked, sipped from his bottle of medicant.

"For a cough," he said, pointing to the dark bottle with raised lettering on the glass.

"Likely you'll cure your thirst from the same flask," cracked Pat.

"Pat, why don't you take a nap," said Alice. "You're awful tired."

He *was* tired. He looked out the window, heaved a sigh. The land shimmered with heat. Off to the right, sunlight glinted on something metallic, silver. He blinked his eyes. Looked again. The stage slowed, pulling a grade. The metal was moving, passed out of his line of sight.

He sat up straight, stuck his head out the window. The hill was steeper than he thought. Ahead he saw nothing but huge boulders lining the road. The air smelled of horse sweat and mesquite.

"What is it, Pat?" Alice asked.

"Nothing. Probably nothing." He paused. "I don't know."

The horses strained to pull the coach up the grade. It was slow going, but the dust wasn't so bad inside the coach. The passengers could hear Swensen yelling at the animals, cracking his whip over their heads.

Pat stuck his head out the window again. The summit was not far off. Another three hundred yards. He could no longer see over the top. Boulders lined both sides of the road. It was a bad spot. He had seen something out there. Something that was not quite right. He didn't like it. But there was no need to worry Alice. And the drummer didn't have much of a brain. What he did have was pickled in alcohol.

Pat's hand slid to his sidearm. He loosened the Colt Peacemaker in its holster. Just in case. Then he leaned back out, looked up at the shotgunner. He saw part of his leg, an arm, the sawed-off Greener held loosely in his hand. Neil Yates didn't appear worried from the way he sat. Pat shrugged.

"What do you keep looking out there for?" his wife asked.

"Just seeing how far we had to go to clear the grade," he lied.

He stubbed out his cigar, stuck the remainder in his shirt pocket. He might have seen quartz glinting in the sun or flakes of mica embedded in the rocks. He doubted either possibility, but there was no use worrying over nothing. He restrained himself from looking outside the coach again. At least he and Alice were facing forward. The drummer faced the rear, his rumpled clothes sweat-soaked, rimmed here and there with rosy dust.

The Concord topped the rise and came to a dead stop.

The passengers were pitched from their seats. The drummer toppled onto the floor. Alice bounced atop him. Pat shot into the opposite seat, striking his head on the leather cushion backing. Dazed, he reached out for the holding strap.

Voices, abrupt, loud, stern, carried to the inside of the coach.

"You climb down off'n that seat, gunner," Parsons said.

"Keep your hands high, driver," Curly said, wearing a wig under his wide-brimmed Stetson.

"Toss down that strongbox," Luke Trask ordered. "Be quick, or be dead!"

Pat clamped a hand over Alice's mouth as she opened her mouth to scream. He grabbed one arm and helped her to her seat. Homer Morrison grumbled, looked up at a bare thigh where Alice's skirt had pulled up over her leg.

"What the hell's going on?" he blurted.

"Shut up!" Pat said, drawing his six-gun.

Alice looked at her husband in stark terror.

"Hold up," Pat whispered. He pulled the side curtains, plunging them into darkness stippled with sunlight. Dust motes twinkled in the still air.

They heard the strongbox crash to the ground.

"Ain't you Curly Brocius?" asked the shotgunner, Yates.

"Shut up!" Trask snapped. Then: "Curly, open up that coach."

Pat tensed.

The door opened, creaking on its hinges.

Alice drew back in fright. Morrison paled beneath the glow of his cheeks. Pat held his pistol low, snug against his leg.

"Come on outa there," Curly said. "Move!"

Pat nodded to Alice and she climbed out first, unassisted. Curly backed off. Pat went out the other door.

Morrison panicked and instead of following Alice out, he threw himself out the other door, right behind Jennings.

Unnerved, Curly fired a shot into the coach. He fired twice more. Alice jerked at each sound. She was in the line of fire.

Trask rode up on the side where Jennings and Morrison had come out, waving a Winchester. The bluing was gone from the barrel. It reflected dazzling light in the sun. He wore a bandanna over his face.

Homer Morrison stared at Trask through blurry eyes. He crouched, pointed a finger.

"I know you!" he shouted. "Trask! From Ellsworth—"

Trask shot him in the throat.

A spray-cloud of blood sparkled in the air as the bullet ripped through the larynx before exploding the spine into splintered bone fragments. Homer Morrison's scream was choked off. His legs danced crazily as his head flopped to his shoulders, the sightless eyes fixed in a glazed stare.

Pat stood, held his arm straight out, and hammered back the Colt .45. He squeezed the trigger.

But Trask was moving, spurring his horse straight at Jennings. The shot missed.

Trask jacked a fresh shell in the chamber, threw his

arm straight out, and squeezed the rifle's trigger. It went off with a roar in Pat's face. Orange flame scorched the air. Black powder struck his face. The bullet, on a downward path, struck him in the shoulder, skidded off bone and tore through ribs, ripped the lung sac in its flight downward. The lead ball lodged in his hip.

Pat twisted away in pain.

"Come on, Curly," Trask shouted. "Let's ride."

Parsons rode up, leered at Alice. Curly grabbed up the strongbox and rode off while the other two men covered him.

Alice rushed to her husband's side.

Alf Swensen came down beside her.

"He ban hurt purty bad," he said. "Ve get him in the coach."

The air exploded as Neil Yates fired both barrels of the Greener after the fleeing horsemen.

They were out of range.

He swung down from the seat, came to help Alf.

"They got away," he said.

"Help me, Neil, by golly. This man ban hurt purty bad, I t'ink."

"Alice," Pat croaked. "I . . . I'm dying. Tell Chad. It was Luke Trask."

"Please," she begged. "Don't go, Pat. I need you. Lucinda needs you." Her face was pale, her voice trembling with fear.

Pat's eyes closed. He shuddered. His eyes opened again, frosted over with the pale cast of death.

"I'm coming," he whispered to no one.

And he was gone.

Alice collapsed over him, sobbing.

That's when Neil and Alf noticed the blood on her back.

CHAPTER FOURTEEN

Hector sighed. His ears hurt. One in particular—his right ear. That's the side Gabriela Gomez had sat on all the way from Nogales in the northbound. A constant stream of talk. Questions. He had answered them all a dozen times. How had her father died? Why wasn't Morgan there to help him? What was going to be done about it? Why did he work for gringos? How far was the Jennings ranch? Endless. Tiring. Questions, *hijo de mala leche, preguntas y preguntas!*

Gabriela was petite, with raven-black hair, nut-brown eyes, pear-shaped as a fawn's, spit curls dangling next to her ears, a mantilla of black lace on her head, full lacy dress, high-heeled, lace-up boots. She looked like a grandee's lady. A mole was next to her full lips and she had breasts that pushed against her bodice with the persistence of pouter pigeons strutting a mating dance.

"We will be there soon," he said, stepping from the coach. The stage had pulled up in Benson, where he'd left the spring wagon and the dappled gray. "It is only a very few short little miles."

He helped her down. They were the only two passengers, since the stageline carried mostly freight from the East to the border towns. It was to meet the Tucson stage, then return by way of Tombstone.

"Hector, do not forget the luggage," Gabriela commanded.

"I will not forget." He looked up helplessly at the two men on the buck seat. One of them crawled back and grabbed the two valises. One was a large carpetbag, the other of worn leather. He grunted from the effort.

"Be careful," Gabriela said in English. "Do not break anything."

"Yes, ma'am," the man said sarcastically. "What've you got in here? Gold?"

"My dowry," she said in precise English, her words only slightly accented. She turned to Hector and blistered him in a stream of liquid Spanish. He dutifully walked over to where the men could hand down Gabriela's luggage. He nearly collapsed under the weight of the leather suitcase. The carpetbag put him on his knees. Gabriela was not amused. He brushed off the dust as he set the bag down.

"I will get the spring wagon," he said. "It's at the livery."

"Be quick about it. I need a bath. I'm weary. I'm hungry and thirsty."

"Por seguro," Hector muttered, lugging the heavy bags to the porch of the freight office. He puffed with exertion and streaked a pair of fingers across his fore-

head, pushing back his sombrero, and the stream of sweat flew into the air.

A man came out of the freight office. He was short, barrel-chested, phlegmatic. His legs were bowed and he wore an old, converted percussion pistol in a worn hide holster. His hat was Montana-crimped, soiled with the stains of careless living.

"Hold on thar," he said to Hector, who had started to cross the street.

Gabriela fanned her face furiously with impatient winglike strokes.

"Yes, señor?"

"You Hector Salcedo?"

The Mexican nodded, his eyebrows raised in quizzical semicircles.

"You get on over to Doc Patterson's pronto."

"What is the trouble?" Hector asked.

"Doc and the marshal will tell you all about it, *amigo*. He's the next street over, next to the Grange."

"I know where he is," Hector said politely.

"I will go with you," Gabriela said. To the man who had spoken to Hector, she said, "Please watch my bags while we are gone."

"Yes'm," the man said, turning on his heel and returning to the office.

Gabriela shot him a dark look, but stepped quickly to catch up with Hector, who was turning into the walkway between the freight office and the barbershop.

There was a crowd in front of Patterson's, whose modest office was crowded in among a number of false fronts. Wagons lined the street. Men and women milled, chattered, gaped as Hector and Gabriela threaded their way through the crowd.

"Was it Curly Bill?" someone asked Neil Yates.

"Meanest man I ever saw," Yates said, nodding.

"Alf, did you see who the others were?" asked a man with a butcher's apron swaddling his waist.

"They wore handkerchiefs over their faces, *ja*," Swensen said.

"Let's get up a posse!" an inebriated young man yelled, a three-day beard bristling his face.

Hector went inside, followed by Gabriela.

A small knot of men stood in the anteroom talking in low tones. One of them wore a badge that proclaimed: U. S. Deputy Marshal. He looked at the pair who had entered, separated from the group of men.

"You Hector Salcedo?"

Hector nodded.

"We got word from Pearblossom's you was due in today. Good thing, too." Pearblossom's was the livery stable. "You work for Pat Jennings?"

"Yes."

"He got shot. Dead. The missus is in with the sawbones. Wants to see you. Who's the lady?"

"This is—" Hector began.

"I'm Gabriela Maria Gomez y Martinez," Gabriela said, interrupting. "I am on my way to see the Jennings."

The marshal looked bewildered. His slate eyes swept Gabriela up and down, then closed in exasperation. "I'm Marshal Barker," he said. "Preston Barker. You two come with me." He was a mustached, lean man in his forties with pale-gray eyes.

The deputy ushered them through the door into the doctor's office. A woman met them and led them to a screen that blocked off part of the room. Alice Jennings lay on a large bed built against the wall. She was very pale.

Doc Patterson was bent over her, listening to her heart through a stethoscope. He saw Barker and shook his head somberly. Alice's eyes were closed. Her breathing was very shallow. A white sheet was pulled up to her neck. The doctor removed the stethoscope from under the sheet and stuck the listening end into the pocket of his gray smock. "You Hector?" he whispered.

Hector stared numbly at Mrs. Jennings. He took off his hat, worried the brim in both hands. Gabriela looked at the woman on the bed with sharp, glittering eyes.

"She wants to talk to you. I'm Cecil Patterson. There's not much time. Deputy, take the lady into my office."

Gabriela shook off his hand as Barker touched her arm.

"I will stay," she said evenly. The doctor nodded, his brown eyes expressionless. He was a thin rail of a man with a hooked nose, pince-nez, graying sideburns. He wore black pin-striped trousers under the smock, polished brown shoes.

Patterson leaned over Alice and whispered something in her ear.

Alice's eyelids fluttered, slid back as her eyes opened. "Hector?" she murmured. "Is that you?"

"*Sí, patrona,* I am here," Hector said. Deputy Barker nudged him toward the bed.

Alice reached out a hand, took his.

"I am sorry, señora."

"Hector, listen to me." Her voice was a dry cornhusk rustled by the wind. Her forehead was clammy with sweat. The doctor dabbed it with a piece of rolled-up gauze. "Pat is gone. He was killed by Luke Trask. Tell Chad Morgan."

The marshal leaned forward, listening intently.

"I will tell him," Hector said quietly.

"My purse. Take that to Lucinda. There is money in it. Tell her I love her."

"I will bring her here," Hector said defiantly. "I will hurry."

The squeeze on his hand was weak.

Alice tried to shake her head, winced.

"No. I . . . I won't be here tomorrow," she said. "In a little while . . ."

Tears stung Hector's eyes, rolled down his cheeks. He squeezed her hand as if to give her some of his strength.

"That's all, son," Patterson said quietly. "I'll talk to you in my office. Deputy?"

This time Gabriela did not push his hand away as Barker took her arm. Hector's lips quivered as if there was something more he wanted to say. Alice shuddered. Her eyes closed. Hector turned away as he heard her throat rattle with sound. The doctor bent over Alice quickly, jerking the sheet away from her bare chest.

A few moments later, he entered his office. "She's gone," he told Hector. "I think she just stayed alive long enough to talk to you. Wouldn't say a word to us."

"I'm mighty interested in what she said," the marshal said. "What was that about Chad Morgan? You know where he is, Salcedo?"

136

A wary look crept into Hector's eyes. "I do not know," he lied.

"Well, we got a flier up from Tombstone today. And a note from Sheriff Rushmore saying Chad Morgan murdered his family. I got to look into that. You hold anything back from me and I—"

"Please, Deputy," Patterson said, removing his pince-nez and wiping them with the tail of his smock. "This is hardly the time or place for an inquisition. Mrs. Jennings is dead. You have other duties to perform."

"What happened?" Gabriela asked. "Was she shot?"

Hector was numb, staring at the floor. His shoulders sagged under the weight of what he had just experienced.

"Yes," the doctor said. "She sustained severe internal injuries from two gunshot wounds. The woman was brave and strong. I understand her husband succumbed at the scene."

"The stage was robbed," Deputy Barker said. "By three men. One of them, we think, was Curly Bill Brocius. What was that about a Trask? A Luke Trask?" He skewered Hector with a look.

"I don't know who that is," Hector said honestly. "I must go to the house now and tell Señora Jennings's daughter. This is very bad. Very bad. I do not feel so good."

Gabriela took his arm. "We will go now," she said. "Thank you, Doctor."

"The remains will be over to the mortuary," Patterson said. "Miss Jennings can come over in the morning to tell Tillman, the undertaker, what she wants done. I'll fill out the death certificates right away."

The marshal nodded to the doctor, walked to the anteroom with Gabriela and Hector. The nurse was out there, visiting with the other men.

"You can all go outside now," the marshal ordered. "I got business here. Miss Merrill, you go on back in. The doc needs you."

When the room was cleared, Deputy Barker looked sternly at Hector. "I'll be out to look around, Salcedo," he said. "There's something funny going on and I think you know a lot more'n you're telling."

"No, sir. I don't know nothing."

"Be that as it may, I'm bound to look into this matter. Was Chad Morgan in with those holdup men?"

"No!"

"Well, what do you know about his family? He kill 'em, like it says?"

"No. I do not think so."

"Well, you must know something."

Gabriela stepped up, then, glared at the marshal.

"Marshal, he's told you what you asked. Do not bully this man anymore. We will go now." Gabriela was small, but she stood up on her tiptoes to give authority to her words. The marshal licked his lips as if trying to decide whether to answer her or let them go.

He threw up his hands. "You," he said to Hector. "Don't you go anywhere unless you check with me. I may be out there tonight or in the morning. Now go on. I got work to do."

Hector sighed with relief. Gabriela took his arm, led him outside.

"Thank you, Señorita Gomez," he said gratefully. "I am in shock. Poor Señora Jennings. Poor Señor Pat."

138

"Come on, Hector," she said, whisking him through the whispering crowd out front. "You are a very poor liar. You whine too much in the face of authority. Now, where is this Chad Morgan? My father wrote much about him."

"You will meet him, I think," Hector said.

"He is at the ranch where we are going?"

"Yes."

"Good. We must help him to escape. Unless he really is a murderer."

"No, he is not a murderer. But he is very sick. He has been shot. I think, by this man Luke Trask."

Gabriela swore.

Hector looked at her in shock. A convent girl, speaking such words. It was not right.

"Oh, come on, Hector," Gabriela said, "you have heard the words before. Do not be fooled by appearances."

"But the convent . . . the sisters . . ."

"That was my father's idea. Do you think we girls just sat around and prayed all day? Come on, let's get to the livery before your face freezes and falls off."

Twenty minutes later, the spring wagon bumped and bounced on the road to the Jennings ranch. Gabriela's baggage lay in the back.

CHAPTER FIFTEEN

Lucinda Jennings saw the wagon coming from a long way off. A spool of dust funneled into the air. "Someone's coming," she called to Chad Morgan. "I think it's Hector, and the Gomez girl."

Morgan hobbled to the door, using a stick as a makeshift cane. He did not want to put much weight on his hips, but he felt stronger than he had in days. He had soaked in a hot tub that morning and then sat in the sun for an hour. The new flesh had started to push through the bullet holes, pink and tender. But the seepage was gone, the edges of the wounds toughened up like hide dried in the sun.

"Maybe it's your folks," he said.

"No, that's the spring wagon. They'd be in the surrey."

Morgan saw that she was right.

"Hector must be in a hell of a hurry," he said.

"There you go, swearing again. I declare, Chad, you're a caution!"

They watched as the wagon rumbled up into the

yard. Hector's face was pale under the thin film of dust. Gabriela Gomez sat very stiff on the seat next to him. Hector sat there, staring at Lucinda. Gabriela punched his arm, said something to him.

"Something's up," Morgan said instinctively.

Gabriela stood up, slapped her dress with flat hands. Dust puffed from the dress. She climbed down and marched to the porch. Hector sat there, still. He removed his hat, began wringing it in both hands.

"Señorita Jennings. I am Gabriela Gomez. And you must be Chad Morgan," she said with a nod to Chad. "Miss Jennings, Hector has swallowed his tongue, so I must be the one to inform you that your parents have been killed. Forgive me for bringing you this bad news. I am so sorry."

Lucinda's face fell. Then, a look of disbelief washed over her features. She gasped for breath. The blood drained from her face and her knees buckled. Chad stepped to her side, put an arm around her for support.

Lucinda looked at Hector for confirmation. He nodded solemnly.

"Oh, no!" she shrieked.

Gabriela rushed up to her.

"I will take her inside," she said to Morgan, who looked at Gabriela dumbfounded as the Mexican girl grasped Lucinda's arms and led her inside the house. He stood there for a long moment, frowning.

"Hector, you'd better explain all this to me before we go in," he said to the Mexican who climbed down from the spring wagon sheepishly. He pulled the dappled gray over to the hitch rail, slung the reins over it. Stumbling over his words, he blurted out the news of

141

the stage holdup, the shootings, the last moments of Alice Jennings. Tears flowed copiously from his eyes.

"That's a hell of a note," Morgan said.

Hector looked over his shoulder. "And this Marshal Barker will be out here to arrest you very soon, I think."

"He'll play hob," Morgan said, his face hardening. "Come on inside."

"No, I will bring in the baggage and unhitch the horse. Do you want me to saddle Captain Joe?"

Morgan considered it. He nodded. He was not ready to ride yet, but it appeared that he had no choice. Trask had to be stopped and he didn't have time to argue with a U. S. marshal. He turned and went inside the house—to the sound of sobbing.

Both women were weeping. They sat on the overstuffed couch, their arms around each other.

Morgan hobbled to a chair, stretched out his legs. "I'm damned sorry, Lucinda," he said.

She looked at him with tear-filled eyes. "Must you always swear? At a time like this, especially! Oh, Chad, what am I going to do?"

He knew she was raving at him out of grief. And somehow he felt responsible. Trask had dogged his trail for years and now, in this short span of time, he had murdered the people closest to him. It didn't make sense. Was it a quirk of fate or a deliberate plan of diabolical proportions? He let her words wash over him. There had to be some way for the grief, the anger, the hatred to come out. Reason would follow when she found the calm after the storm.

"It's not easy, Lucinda," he said quietly. "I'll help all I can."

Gabriela fixed him with taloned eyes. "Did Hector tell you what they are saying?" she asked. "That you murdered your wife, your son, and my father?"

"Yes."

"What?" asked Lucinda. "That's not true."

Gabriela assessed Morgan with her eyes. Looked him up and down.

"Can you ride?" she asked.

"I reckon. If I have to."

"We must go to Benson early in the morning. I would like to go to my father's grave, but that can wait. What will you do, Chad Morgan?"

He hadn't quite put a notch in Gabriela's ear yet. She was a puzzle. She got right to the point. What was he going to do? Lucinda needed him. Gabriela, too, probably. But if he went to town with them, he was liable to walk right into the hoosegow.

He was beginning to feel like he'd been ridden hard and put away wet. He was strong enough to travel if he took it easy. He needed another month or so before he would feel topnotch. He didn't have another month, let alone two. Trask was out there somewhere. Trask had caused all this grief. The man had bad blood, and now it was affecting them all. He had to be stopped, put down—down deep.

"If you think you can manage, I'll be riding," he told Gabriela. "To Tombstone."

"That is a good idea. You will hunt the man down who murdered all these people?"

"Yes. I will hunt him down."

Lucinda pulled away from Gabriela's embrace. "You can't!" she said. "You're not strong enough! Stay here. I . . . we'll hide you out."

Morgan shook his head. "I can't stay. I've caused you enough trouble, Lucinda. And you, too, Miss Gomez."

"My name is Gabriela," she said. "Did Hector tell you that the sheriff in Tombstone was looking for you?"

"No, but it figures. Trask—or a man named Parsons—must have spread the story about me. What can you tell me about the holdup? I reckon it just happened the Jennings were on the wrong stage at the wrong time."

"I do not know much. They say there were three men. One of them was named Curly. And Trask, of course."

"Curly? Any last name?"

"It was Brocius," said Hector, puffing in with Gabriela's valises. He dropped them to the floor with a thud. "Why?"

"Oh, nothing," said Morgan. "Curly's getting to be a common name in these parts, that's all."

He'd heard of Curly Bill Brocius, of course—mean as a sidewinder—but he couldn't figure Bill Brocius and Trask hooking up. Not when Brocius was at odds with the Earps and thick with the Clanton clan. And if Trask had taken that stage, there should have been four men, including Brocius. Parsons and Higgins, Trask and Brocius. It was a puzzle. Brocius had his own bunch. And Trask was every bit the leader Curly Bill was. Two men leading a three-man holdup team? In a pig's squint eye!

"Chad," Lucinda said, "I'm sorry I laced into you. You didn't deserve that. You've got your cross to bear, too."

144

"Don't mention it, Lucinda." Morgan stood up. "You saddle my horse, Hector?"

"Sí. She is ready. I have tied him in the back." Except for his pronouns, Morgan thought, Hector spoke pretty fair English.

"Good. I'll be obliged if I can get some jerky and hardtack to stick in my saddlebags. I might be a few days getting to Tombstone the roundabout way."

"Are you going there now?" Lucinda asked, the faintest trace of a whine in her voice.

"Soon. But there's something else I have to do first. I think you three can manage without me. I'm sorry I can't go to the funeral, but I better keep away from the hobbles right now. Lucinda, can you and Hector do a little lying for me?"

"I don't understand," Lucinda said.

"Listen. Both of you. I want you to tell the marshal and anybody else who asks that I didn't make it. You say that a bastard name of Fred Parsons shot me in the back and you buried me next to my wife and son."

"How can that be?" Lucinda asked.

"I'll take care of it. That'll be my first stop. I'll just put up another grave and tack my name on it real proper."

"You can't be serious."

"It'll hold Barker off for a while."

"I should go with you," Gabriela said. "I want to see my father's grave."

"No. You stay with Lucinda. She'll need you. Give me a week or so, and I'll be in Tombstone. If you need me, I'll take a room at the Russ House. Do you know it?"

145

The three other people in the room shook their heads.

"It's on the corner of Fifth and Tough Nut streets. If I'm not there, I'll be found at either the Tivoli or the Capitol Saloon. The Tivoli is on Allen. The Capitol's at Fourth and Fremont. At Russ House, I'll register under the name of F.B. Anvic."

"Who's that?" asked Lucinda.

"My grandpa on my mother's side."

Morgan smiled. He looked at the stick in his hand. He picked it up and broke it across his knee.

"Here," he said to Hector, handing him the splintered pieces, "use this for kindling. I won't be needing it anymore."

"Before you go," Lucinda said, "there's something I want to give you. You'll need it and I know Pa would want you to have it."

She walked over to the fireplace and reached up over the mantel. She took down the new Winchester rifle, handed it to Morgan.

He looked at it and at her.

"Thanks," he said. "I'll be mighty proud to own it." He put his arms around Lucinda, drew her close. She trembled against him.

Gabriela's eyes narrowed. She pulled absentmindedly on a spit curl, took a deep breath.

"Good-bye," Morgan said.

He had to tear himself out of Lucinda's arms.

Gabriela was still looking at him with hooded eyes when he left a half hour later, canteens full, grub in his saddlebags, the new Winchester in his boot.

"I will see you in Tombstone," she whispered to him, out of earshot of Lucinda and Hector.

"You don't have to . . ."

"I am alone," she said. "I have no family. I will be there. At Russ House."

Something spidery crawled on the back of his neck. Gabriela and Lucinda were orphans now. Somehow, he felt responsible. But Gabriela surprised him. She was a tenacious sort. There was weight to her words. A weight he didn't understand. Didn't want to. He looked into her eyes, trying to fathom their depths. They glittered like agates. They were steady on his. Persistent.

"Tombstone's a rough town."

"I know. All of the gringo towns are rough. And they do not grow enough flowers. I want to be with you, Chad Morgan. You are all that is left of my father. You were his friend. I am his daughter, but I did not know him. Please. Let me be close to you. For a while." Tears misted her eyes. She blinked them away. Her chin quivered.

"Suit yourself," he said roughly, aware of Gabriela's eyes on him. He broke away from her, gently pulled himself up into the saddle. A twinge of pain tugged at his leg when he swung it over the cantle.

He waved to the women and Hector. Captain Joe felt good under him. He swung north toward his former home, where he would dig his own grave.

Morgan finished driving in the crude cross at the head of the mound of stones.

The lettering on it read: CHAD MORGAN. Born October 20, 1857. Died May 3, 1882. Killed by Fred Parsons.

There were crosses on the other graves now, too.

He picked up his shirt, wiped his face before putting it back on.

The sun was almost spent for the day, but there was more to do. He raked a cedar broom over all of the tracks he had made. If the marshal showed up today, or soon, he would not find any fresh signs that he had been there. If he thought Chad Morgan was dead, that would give him more time. He might tell Henry Rushmore, mayor and sheriff of Tombstone, that he could close the wanted file on him. He might.

Morgan had cut the cedar branch long enough so that he could drag it behind his horse when he left.

Captain Joe spooked at the strange object draped over his rump but soon grew accustomed to the bristly branch as Morgan rode him away from the burnt-out remains of what had once been his home. The horse was in good condition, well rested, well fed. He had a lot of bottom to him. It was ironic, Morgan thought, that he wouldn't be putting the animal to the test. The ride from the Jennings ranch had been slow and tiring. After the exertion of piling stones on the fake grave, he could feel the tugs of pain in the wounds. His right leg was weak, tired. His lower back ached. It felt as if a leaden sack was weighting him down, sapping him of vitality, strength.

He rode to the high ground, trying not to look back, trying to shut out the memories of the last hours of his family's life. In a few minutes, he was glad he had chosen that course, rather than taking the easier way across the flat of his former ranch.

A trail of dust, an eighth of a mile long, drifted up in the air on the road that led to the ranch. The dust hung there like a sorrel mare's tail fanned by a wind but frozen in the dying rays of the falling sun.

Morgan let the cedar broom fall to the ground. He stepped his horse carefully so as not to raise any dust. He rode for cover in the rocks. There, he dismounted and crawled to a vantage point.

The riders were closer. Strung out for that eighth of a mile. A dozen of them, at least.

Morgan knew who they were, without knowing their names.

Even as he watched, the one in front raised a hand, moved it right and left.

The riders in the rear began to fan out, form an encircling pincer.

The man in front would be the U. S. marshal. Barker.

The others went by a single name.

Posse!

CHAPTER SIXTEEN

Tombstone lay sprawled across the treeless plateau, like a basking Gila in the late afternoon. Spanish bayonets and frayed yucca, a grave or two, a shed, were the only breaks in the monotony until one reached the clutter of clapboards and soddies that marked the town itself. Low hills in the distance scarred the skyline. A single mound at the far end of town, beyond the last shack, furnished the only cover for a man approaching who didn't want to be seen right away.

Morgan waited behind the hump on the plateau, a sodden bandanna draped over his forehead.

He sat in Captain Joe's shade, listening for any alien sound, waiting for the late-afternoon sun to fall behind the far mountains.

He had changed a lot in the three weeks he had been traveling, eluding the posse that dogged his heels.

He had some respect for Marshal Barker, who was almost as good a tracker as he was himself. Almost.

There had been times when Morgan was certain that

he had lost him, but when he awoke, there was that trail of dust, like a mare's tail, hanging in the sky.

Once he had lost the posse for a week.

He had holed up, letting his flesh knit together, feeling that the danger was over. Rifle shots had startled him out of sleep. Not aimed at him. The posse hunting game. They, too, were hard men determined, like Barker, to bring him in.

So, the false grave had not fooled them.

Chad had watched as they tore it to pieces, like dogs fighting over a single fowl, and heard their whoops when they had found no corpse. That's when he had made tracks out of there. Not toward Benson or Tombstone, but toward the Dragoons, the only haven he was likely to have. And someone in that party knew the Dragoons. They knew where every *tenaje* was, every spring. He had led them to alkali wells and over steep, treacherous ridges. He had doubled back on them, circled, ridden their flanks. No rest, little sleep. Just dry food and lizards to eat. He was slimmed down and hard as tempered steel.

Finally, a week ago, he had eluded them.

Luck. Pure luck.

The herd of wild horses had saved his bacon. He had chased them for miles, staying in their clutter of tracks. Finally, he had scattered them on a sun-baked dry lake bed where the wind swept the tracks away as fast as a man could make them. There the clay had hardened into stone, the alkali-caked mud had cracked a century ago and each fissure had widened over the years. It was a no-man's-land of heat and blistering winds—five miles of hell, where there wasn't a trace of life or the track of man or beast.

Now, he was close to Tombstone, close enough to ride in under cover of darkness and slip into a new identity. His beard was thick on his face, his face leaner than before. His wounds were nearly fully healed, the new pink flesh now taking on the coloration of his skin, rising in darker-colored bumps out of the bullet holes.

Hunger gnawed at his innards. Captain Joe was showing rib bones, his flanks caved in from lack of grain. His coat was shabby, caked with mud, dust, alkali, and bleeding from blow flies. A sorry sight, the both of them. Morgan's eyes were red-rimmed, scratched by the wind and fine dust, weary from lack of sleep. Yet one thought had kept him going, given him strength.

Get Trask!

And, after Trask, Parsons and Higgins.

The sun had been hot all day, but the western sky was already darkening with furled clouds blowing in from the northwest. The dawn had been bloodred and all day the wind had been circling, sniffing at his back, then blowing into his face. Strong gusts had peppered his face with fine grit, stung his face and eyes. Now, the promise of the red morning was in the ominous sunset building west of the town. There would be rain before morning—a frog-strangler unless he missed his guess, maybe even before he left the safety of the hill and started into town.

The wind freshened and he felt the change. The chill in the air. The dampness. He took the bandanna from his forehead, squeezed the moisture out. Captain Joe bristled, perked his ears. His nostrils flared as he sniffed the quick gust of wind that fanned his mane from the northwest.

Red sky at morning.

He knew the sailor's term.

Take warning.

Rains came sudden to that arid land, he knew. Flash floods had washed many a rider into the grave, many a horse, many a beef.

He stood up, marked the sun's position. He held up a pair of fingers, aligned them horizontally between the sun and the horizon. One finger was enough. Less than fifteen minutes before sunset. A fluttering in his stomach. A feather scraping across the back of his neck. A razor sawing across the nerves in his brain.

Soon, he would be in Tombstone.

That's where the danger was.

But that's where Luke Trask might be, too.

Parsons and Higgins, as well.

The killers of his wife and son. Killers of Tío Pedro.

Killers he would kill.

He caught up Captain Joe's reins. "Come on, boy. Let's get to it."

Morgan swung into the saddle, circled the small hill and headed for Tombstone. The sun was down, buried beyond the clouds, the far mountains. The shadows deepened, the lights winked on in the town. Morgan rode slowly, letting the darkness deepen.

He heard horses, the low talk of men: miners riding down out of the hills to slake their thirsts, seek the company of painted women; ranchers coming into town to swap lies at a saloon or sit at the tables bucking the tiger at faro, or playing three-card monte, poker, at places where the law looked the other way.

At Fifth and Tough Nut, he pulled up to Russ House, dismounted, and wrapped the reins around the hitch rail. He went inside, boots muffled on the carpet in the lobby. The clerk looked up, frowned. Men and women looked out from behind rattling sheets of newsprint on the *Epitaph* and *Nugget*, sniffing the stranger out. Morgan ignored them. He heard footsteps on the stairs, coming down.

"I'd like a room," he told the clerk. "A weekly rate if I can get it. Point me to a bath while you're at it."

"Bath's down the hall. One ahead of you. Seven dollars for the room, in advance. Bath's two bits."

The clerk opened the register, shoved it at Morgan.

The man came down the stairs, saw Morgan and grinned. He walked over to the desk. Morgan saw him. Recognition flooded his features.

"Why, hello there, Mister . . ." the young man blurted out before Morgan cut him off.

"Rudy!" he said. "Rudy Owens."

"Say, you better—"

"Rudy, what're you doing here?" Morgan asked, annoyed. He pushed the money across the desk at the clerk, who was watching the exchange with a puzzled look on his face.

"Me? I'm working in the mines . . . but you?"

"Just come into town. Been south, across the border, chasing longhorns."

Bewildered, Rudy looked at the clerk and at Morgan.

"Billy Niles, this here's—" Rudy said.

"F.B. Anvic," Morgan said coldly. "Out of Yuma."

"Anvic?" Rudy looked at Morgan in puzzlement. Then, seeing the cold look in Morgan's eyes, nodded. "Oh, yeah. F.B. Forgot your handle for a speck there."

"Good to see you, Owens. Come on up to my room and we'll chew some fat."

The clerk wrote something down on his ledger and turned to the cubbyholes for a key.

"Room twelve," he said. "Upstairs, right."

Morgan took the key, muscled Rudy Owens in front of him, up the stairs.

Inside the room, Morgan faced his former employee.

"Sorry, Rudy, I had to ride over you down there. But I'm going by the name of Anvic for a time."

"I didn't think, Mister Morgan. But you're smart. You're wanted by the law here. You didn't—"

"No. Someone else killed Bonnie and little Tommy. And old Tío Pedro Gomez, too."

"Sorry, sir."

"Be pleased if you wouldn't give me away, Rudy. Now you run along. I got to get settled in, put my horse up."

"I won't say nothin'," Rudy said, as if glad to be part of the conspiracy. He looked as if he wanted to say something else, but Morgan ushered him out too fast.

Morgan looked around the room. It was better than the fifteen-cent-a-night fleabags on Allen Street. It had a wooden bed, a highboy, a sideboard with a washbasin, pitcher, two glasses, a table and a couple of chairs. Faded prints hung crookedly on the walls. There were two wall lamps and one on the table. He struck a match, lit it, turning down the wick. The window overlooked Tough Nut Street. It was quiet on the street.

An hour later, after putting up his horse at the livery stable and taking a bath, shaving off a month's beard, except for the mustache, he dropped his key off at the

155

desk. Billy Niles, the clerk, looked up over rimless spectacles and blinked.

"Oh, Mister Anvic, it's you. You got a message. I plumb forgot about it when you checked in."

Niles rummaged around in the papers behind the counter, came up with a small, sealed envelope.

"Lady said to give it to you when you checked in. But that was several days back."

"Thanks," Morgan said, taking the envelope. The clerk stared at him, neck craning, but Morgan didn't open it. Instead, he folded it, stuck it in his belt.

Morgan had one pair of serviceable trousers in his bedroll and a shirt that wasn't worn clean through, but both fit him loosely and he knew he'd have to find new duds in the morning. For now, the clothes gave him a nondescript look, an anonymity that suited him. The money from the cattle sale would tide him over for a long while, so he wasn't worried about surviving in Tombstone.

He knew the town well, but it was still growing. He had watched it grow from a tent city to a clapboard town, and now it glittered with fancy restaurants and hotels, respectable businesses. Underneath, though, it was still a tough town, proud of its mean reputation ever since the eastern papers and magazines had exploited the shoot-out at the O.K. Corral, in October, two years before.

He walked down Fifth Street to Allen, the roughest street in Tombstone. Gunfire erupted as brawls broke out. Hoarse yells could be heard coming from the dance halls and saloons that flourished after the commercial district closed down for the day. The town itself boasted that Allen Street furnished "a dead man for breakfast every morning." Morgan was not yet ready to show his face in the Tivoli or the Capitol. First, there was a man he wanted to see. The only friend he knew he could count on in Tombstone.

The dim-lit Tecolote Cantina was set back off the street. A faded sign hung at right angles to the false front featuring a large picture of an owl under the name. Morgan went inside, sweeping the large single room with a glance. A man plucked a guitar in one corner. A few Mexicans sat at the bar, begrimed, sipping *mezcal* and *cerveza*.

The barkeep glanced up, looked down, then looked up again.

"José," Morgan said. *"Que tal, hombre?"*

José Mendoza grinned wide, tossed down his towel and limped around the bar. He pumped Morgan's hand, shaking it. Then, he looked around furtively, and led the tall man to an empty table next to a wall decorated with a faded bullfight poster.

"You should not be in here, *amigo*," José whispered. "Not in Tombstone. It is not true what they say, but there are many men looking for you."

Quickly, Chad Morgan told his friend that he was going under the name of F.B. Anvic and why he was in Tombstone. He told him about the murder of his family and his friend, Pedro Gomez.

José Mendoza listened intently, his dark-brown eyes fixed on Morgan's face. José was a short, barrel-shaped man, with a wooden leg. His eyes were wide-set, his nose bulbous in a moon face. Black hair, cut short, glistened under a felt hat.

"I am looking for a man named Luke Trask," Mor-

157

gan said, "and two others. One is named Parsons, the other is called Higgins."

"This Trask. I know him. He is found at the Golden Bull these days—now that he has much money. He lives at the Lone Wolf when he is in town. I do not know this Parsons, nor the other man."

"The Golden Bull?"

"It is a new place. It is near Fourth, on Allen Street."

"Thanks," Chad said as he glanced around the room. "You are doing well, José?"

"Thanks to you. The cantina is my life. And my daughter's."

"Carmen? She must be—"

"She has eighteen years now. She is in back, making the tortillas, cooking the beans. I know what it is to lose a woman. But Carmen has done her best to take care of this old man."

José had worked for Morgan three years ago. He had been a good *vaquero*, but a bad fall had splintered the bones in his leg. The leg had threatened to turn gangrenous when Morgan had cut it off, saving the man's life. He had staked José to the cantina. Carmen had been fifteen then. He didn't remember her well. Long legs and dark eyes, black hair. Shy. José had since repaid Morgan. They were friends.

"I'll have some grub," Morgan said, "and I'll ask a favor."

"Anything," José said.

Morgan asked for pencil and paper. José produced both, and Morgan started drawing a picture, writing down numbers. Both men were absorbed in the drawing and Morgan's explanation when a shadow fell across the table.

Morgan looked up. "Carmen?" he said.

"I am Carmen," she answered. "And who are you?"

She was beautiful. The eyes had softened, the skin taken on an olive sheen. Her nose was straight, aquiline, her lips full. Her modest dress could not conceal the sculptured curves, the woman's bosom that fought the bodice. She smelled of mashed corn and wild prairie flowers, of earth and scented soap, delicate perfume.

"Call me Anvic," he said.

She drew back, puzzled.

José slapped her rump.

"It is my old friend, Chad," he whispered. "Chad Morgan."

Carmen's eyes widened. She gave a squeal of delight and threw her arms around Chad, nearly knocking him over. Her lips grazed his and breasts mashed into his chest.

"Little Carmen," he laughed. "You have grown."

CHAPTER SEVENTEEN

Curly Garth threw the ring down on the table. Trask looked up at him, saw the look of anger on the bald-headed man's face.

"You got something stuck in your craw, Curly?"

"She laughed at me," Garth said bitterly. "The bitch laughed at me when I asked her to marry up with me. I showed her the ring, and she said to come back when I got one with a bigger stone. The damned thing's no-account!"

Luke Trask grinned. "Hell, you want to sell it back to me, Curly?"

"Damned right! It's bad luck!"

Trask frowned.

"I'll give you ten dollars for it."

"Twenty."

"Fifteen."

"Hell, fifteen, then, Trask. Take it!"

Trask shelled out fifteen dollars in paper, picked up the ring. The Lone Wolf was quiet, and Trask was dressed to go out on the town. He wore black pin-striped trousers, a new white shirt, fancy kid boots. He picked up the ring, which was now attached to a cheap imitation gold chain. He put the chain around his neck.

"I know a gal might take this, by and by," Trask said. "Seen Parsons around?"

"He's waitin' for you at the Golden Bull. Delbert Harris is looking all over for you, too. He's got some news."

"About Morgan?"

Curly nodded. He stuffed the bills in his pocket, waved to the barkeep for a drink.

"He say anything?" Trask pressed.

"No. Said he wanted to see you, is all."

"I don't like it. Things've been going real good and now Dav—Delbert's got his tail up about something."

"Whiskey," Curly said to the barkeep who had come over. "A bottle."

Trask rose from the table.

"Don't let a gal throw you, Curly. There's plenty of flowers on the prairie. You're still sober in an hour, I'll be at the Bull."

The Golden Bull boasted a gaudy front with a billboard proclaiming Marie Shannon as the "singing thrush of Tombstone" appearing in the Arena Theatre, along with "a bevy of dancing girls and a city orchestra."

Luke Trask shoved through the batwing doors, swaggering with the confidence of hard money and two drinks already under his belt. He held a good cigar in his left hand, the ash a half-inch long. The ring glistened in the light from lamps set on wall hooks and a candled chandelier. The saloon was full, a line of men waiting to enter the Arena Theatre, which was a roped-off section at the rear, with an orchestra platform and a curtained stage. The curtain was painted with advertisements.

Fred Parsons waved to him from a table in the center of the room.

Trask cleared a path in front of him.

Delbert Harris put a hand on his arm, materializing out of a knot of men.

"Trask," he said. "Been lookin' for you."

"Set with me and Fred, Delbert."

Trask looked at the back of Delbert's hand. It was tattooed with the initials D.H. It was stupid, that tattoo. It was why Dave Higgins had to use the name of Delbert Harris—or any other name with those same initials.

Harris took his hand away from Trask's arm, followed him to the table, where Parsons sat waiting.

"What's this all about?" Trask asked when he sat down. Parsons and Harris both wore long looks. Trask flicked his ash on the tabletop and sucked deep on the cigar.

"Been talking to a deputy U. S. marshal, name of Preston Barker. He's been tracking Morgan all over Cochise County and up in the Dragoons. Barker gave his report to Sheriff Rushmore, and I was in on it."

Trask poured a drink from Parsons's bottle into one of the empty glasses on the table. His head was wreathed in cigar smoke. "Get to it, Harris," he said.

"Morgan's in Tombstone."

"Huh?" Trask's mouth dropped open like the seat flap of a pair of long johns. "Where?"

162

Harris shrugged, looked around as if expecting to see the man materialize at any moment.

"Deputy Barker doesn't know. He kept on after the posse give up and said he'd bet pesos to peanuts, Morgan is in Tombstone. Found his tracks on that hill outside of town just after dusk."

"Shit," Trask said, putting the cigar down. He reached in his pocket for a match to chew on. "You ask around, Harris?"

"I got to watch it, Trask. Something about that Barker. He don't look right to me. Man's like a bulldog. Hangs on. Looks right through you. I don't know, he wonders why I ask so many questions. I had to pull back. Sheriff Rushmore, he's in a fit. Said he don't want any more trouble. The Earps are giving him stomach pains."

"Rushmore's a pain," Parsons observed, who had kept silent until now.

Trask looked at Parsons, bit down on the matchstick. "Parsons, you messed up."

"Dammit, Trask, he shoulda been dead. I thought sure as Christ he was dead."

"Yeah, well, he ain't. He's here and he's huntin' us."

"I better get some help, I think." Parsons turned as the orchestra tuned up. The hum of voices got louder as patrons ordered drinks, spoke of the show about to begin on stage.

"Who you got in mind?" Harris/Higgins asked.

"Kyle and Tate," Parsons said. "They're in town, hungry."

"Good," Trask said. "Angus Kyle is fast. Buster Tate

163

will back him up. You got any of them flyers on you, Harris?"

Harris took a sheaf of papers from his coat pocket. Each had a crude likeness of Chad Morgan drawn on it. A copy of the drawing that appeared in an *Epitaph* story about Morgan murdering his family. A story planted by Harris himself.

"Give them these," Trask said, taking a couple of the flyers. "And tell them to shoot the sonofabitch down if he shows his face."

"How much?" Parsons asked.

"Whatever they ask. Fifty, a hundred. Besides the reward."

"It's gone up to five hundred," Harris said. "One other thing, Trask."

"Yeah?"

"That deputy marshal, Barker. He asked about you, too. Thinks you're in with Curly Bill Brocius. Those people on the stage died. The Jennings. They were friends of Chad Morgan's. They, or one of 'em, tagged you and Curly."

Parsons let out a breath of relief.

"You're just full of good news, ain't you, Harris?" Trask sneered, grinding down on the match with his teeth.

Harris got up from the table. "Best we don't meet for a while," he said, looking around the room again. "You know where to reach me. And, Trask, was I you, I'd get rid of that ring. It's going to get you hanged, you're not right careful."

"Fuck you, Harris," Trask said, his eyes gone cold.

"Don't look now, Trask," Harris said, flicking his

164

thumb toward the bar, "but there's Deputy Barker. The tall, thin jasper with the mustache."

Harris walked away, leaving Trask and Parsons staring at Marshal Barker. The man hadn't been there before, Trask knew. He had been looking at that very spot not ten seconds before. Nor had he seen the man come in the saloon. He was like a ghost.

"Relax," Parsons said. "He doesn't know what you look like, Trask."

Trask's eyes narrowed to puffy slits.

"No, Fred. And I don't want him to. He's got to be put down."

"Who's the Mex gal with him, I wonder," Parsons said.

"Who cares, Fred." Trask turned his head away from the marshal. "Get to it. I want him down tonight."

Parsons paled, finished his whiskey.

He didn't like it. He didn't like it a damned bit.

"I don't see him here," Gabriela Gomez said, looking around the room.

"He's damn sure in town, and I aim to flush him out," Barker said.

She looked up at the deputy with fluttering eyes.

"And am I the bait?" she asked, a sarcastic edge to her voice.

"You've been acting mighty peculiar, showing up here all alone . . . asking questions. I figure you know something or you wouldn't be so persistent."

"You're a very smart man, Sheriff."

"Marshal," Barker said stiffly. The girl beside him,

Gabriela Gomez had been walking the street, going into places where she had no business going when he had spotted her. Some backtracking had revealed that she had been in Tombstone for three days, asking about the man whose drawing appeared on the poster printed by the *Epitaph*, owned by John Clum. It was the only likeness of the man he was hunting. The curious part was that the Mexican girl, Miss Gomez, was asking for a man who fit the description of Chad Morgan but the name she used was Anvic.

"You going to tell me who this Anvic feller is?" he asked.

"A friend of mine."

"Is he hiding out Chad Morgan?"

Gabriela suppressed a smile. "Maybe," she said coyly.

Exasperated, Barker started to say something when the orchestra struck up a lively overture. Applause deafened him, drowned the first word out of his mouth.

The curtains slowly opened as the orchestra slid into a theme. A tall woman glided onstage. Her blonde hair cascaded down her back. Threaded with sequins, it caught the candlelight and scintillated. Her eyes were very dark, her lips full, red as cherries. She sang, full-throated, projecting her voice over the now-hushed room. She strolled to the footlights in a flowing organdy gown. She sang to each man in the room, a ballad of heartache and broken love that brought tears to some of the more homesick of the miners.

"Who is she?" Gabriela whispered.

"Marie Shannon," Barker said. "She owns the place."

"She's pretty."

"Yes," Barker said, his eyes never leaving the ample bosom of Marie Shannon.

Gabriela started to drift away from the bar. She saw that the deputy marshal was rapt in his appreciation of the talents of Miss Shannon.

Out of the corner of his eye, Barker saw her move.

Gabriela ran.

"Hey, wait a minute!" Barker shouted.

The girl didn't stop. She ran into a grizzled-faced miner, nearly bowling him over. The man slowed her down.

Barker caught up with her, grabbed her arm. Angry stares and loud whispers arose from the small knot of men nearest the action.

Gabriela whirled and tried to twist free of the marshal's grasp. Men pushed and shoved. The singer darted angry glances from the stage in the direction of the commotion.

"Leave me alone!" Gabriela screamed.

Chairs scraped as men rose from tables. The orchestra faltered. Marie Shannon kept singing, raising her voice above the din. A man stood on a table, unsteadily. The table gave way and he fell to the floor with a crash.

Barker jerked Gabriela's arm.

A man punched him in the ear.

Howling with rage, Barker turned to see who had struck him.

Gabriela saw her chance and took it.

She kicked high and hard. The toe of her shoe rammed into Barker's groin. He cried out with pain, doubled over in agony.

"You little bitch!" he gasped. His fingers released their grip on Gabriela's arm. Recovering her balance, she slid between two men and ran zigzag toward the door.

The orchestra stopped playing.

All eyes followed Gabriela's dash for the batwing doors.

Marie Shannon stood onstage, her hands on her hips, glaring at the fleeing girl.

"Stop her!" Barker yelled, straightening up. "Stop that girl!"

He started after her.

Men blocked his way. He drew his pistol.

"I'm a deputy United States marshal!" he declared. "Out of my way."

He hammered back, held the pistol pointed up in the air. Men glared at him. He triggered a shot. Men scattered as the smoke blossomed into the air. They cleared a path for Barker.

Gabriela ran into a man coming through the door— a bald-headed man.

It was Curly Garth.

She looked up at him.

"Let me by," she hissed. "That man's after me!"

Curly stepped aside. Gabriela shot through the doors. Twenty paces behind her, Barker raced headlong, his pistol still in his hand.

Gabriela ran as fast as she could, the long skirt hampering her. She disappeared across the street between two buildings.

Barker saw her and he saw something else.

A man stepped from the shadows where Gabriela

had disappeared. He carried a double-barreled Greener, he took aim, fired both barrels.

Deputy U. S. Marshal Preston Barker walked right into a cloud of deadly double-ought buck.

CHAPTER EIGHTEEN

Chad Morgan didn't want a woman, but Carmen Mendoza was there, in his room, and he couldn't refuse her. He tried to, but he couldn't.

"It is no good for a man to grieve too long," she soothed. "It digs him out inside, makes him hollow. Look at my father. Look at all the widow-men. I have tried to get my father to take another wife, but he won't. He grieves for my mother and he thinks that his one leg prevents him from being a whole man. It is not true. There are women who would love him, who would give him anything he wanted."

"Carmen, I'm not your father."

"I know," she whispered to him, a slinking, purring thing in his arms. She had followed him here after he'd left El Tecolate. Followed him and tapped on the door, stolen inside before he could utter a word of protest.

And now she was offering him her body.

She stood on tiptoe, brushed his lips with hers.

"I like your mustache. Papa said you never wore a mustache before."

"No."

"I like it. I hope you don't shave it off."

Her breasts rubbed against his chest. He felt their heat, the hardness of her nipples.

She was beautiful in the lampglow.

His loins were on fire. But more than that, he wanted to forget his grief for a time. Just as he knew that Carmen wanted temporary relief from her loneliness. She had been alone for a long time. Motherless, a crippled father to worry about.

Morgan could understand. He knew loneliness from the inside now. At every turn of the trail he had missed Bonnie and Tommy. Missed them until his heart hurt to think of them. At times, trying to sleep under the stars, listening for a footfall or hoofbeat, a sign of his relentless pursuers, he had thought that Bonnie and Tommy were still alive, waiting for him to return home. He found himself looking at crimson-smeared sunset skies and thinking that Bonnie would admire them, too.

When he felt Carmen's hand caress the back of his neck, he knew he wanted release from his aching grief.

"Carmen, you've started something. I don't know if I can stop it."

"I don't want you to. It would be cruel. For both of us."

They made love tenderly, passionately, and afterward, they snuggled up to each other on the bed, each of them glowing with the warmth of the other's body.

The shattering thud of fists pounding on the door jerked Morgan to attention. His blood froze.

"Chad! Chad! Let me in! Quick!"

Carmen's startled eyes widened.

It was a woman's voice.

Morgan slid out of bed, grabbed up his trousers. He pulled them on, reached for his pistol. Drew it from the holster.

"Who's that?" Carmen asked.

"I don't know," Morgan said, but the hackles on the back of his neck rose. There was something familiar about the voice. The door shook on its hinges.

"Open the door! Chad, it's me, Gabriela Gomez!"

"Jesus," Morgan muttered, padding barefooted to the door. He glanced back at Carmen who was pulling a sheet up over her nakedness.

He opened the door.

A distraught Gabriela rushed into the room. Her eyes were wide with fright. She was out of breath, panting. Morgan closed the door after checking the hallway. It was empty.

Gabriela saw Carmen in the bed. "Who are you?" she gasped.

"I am Carmen Mendoza." Carmen sat up in bed, drawing the sheet up to her bare shoulders. "I am a friend of Chad Morgan's."

"I see," Gabriela said testily.

She whirled to confront Morgan. "Something terrible's happened. I almost got killed. I saw a murder. Didn't you get my note? Where have you been? Why is this woman here in your room?"

Morgan retreated a step as Gabriela advanced toward him. The pistol was a useless hunk of metal in his hand. He had no place to put it. The room reeked of lovesweat. Gabriela was on the verge of hysteria.

"Hold on," he said to her. "Back off a minute and give it to me slow. Who tried to kill you?"

"Oh!" she exclaimed. "It was horrible! Marshal Barker was chasing me. I ran into this man. He had a gun. He shot the marshal. Killed him, I think."

"You need a drink to calm down. All I have is water."

"Yes, yes, anything."

He shoved his pistol in the holster, poured her a glass of water. She drank it, glaring at Carmen all the while. Morgan saw the note on the floor where it had fallen when he'd taken his pants off. He picked it up, turned up the lamp. He read it quickly.

Dear Chad, it read, *I'm staying here at Russ House. Room 6. I have information for you. Please hurry.* It was signed *Gabriela*.

"I didn't read your note until now," he said. "Sorry."

"If you had, none of this would have happened."

"Tell me about it," he said, leading her to a chair.

Calmer now, Gabriela told him everything that had happened at the Golden Bull.

"Who was the man who shot Barker? Do you know him?"

"Yes."

Carmen was looking at Gabriela with fascination. The sheet had slipped from her chest and she hadn't noticed.

"Who?" Morgan asked.

"Parsons. Fred Parsons. I was with him two hours ago. He told me his name. He . . . he didn't pay me."

173

CHAPTER NINETEEN

Chad Morgan stood in the shadows between the two buildings. There was still a commotion at the Golden Bull, but many of the gawkers had gone back inside to watch the remainder of the show in the Arena Theatre.

He picked up scraps of conversation.

"The man stood right over yonder, blowed that deppity with both barrels. Square in the face."

"Who done it?"

"Feller name of Morgan or Anvic. That one on the poster."

"Barker said they were one and the same afore he cashed in."

"Dirty skulkin' footpad!"

Morgan got the drift. Something Barker had said before he died had made people think he had murdered the deputy. And, from what Gabriela had told him, Barker had already made the connection between Morgan and F.B. Anvic, the name he was using. One thing was in his favor: The mustache he now sported altered his appearance enough so that at first glance no one

174

was likely to recognize him—except Trask. He didn't know about Parsons and Higgins.

The orchestral music floated out on the night air. A woman's voice sang a plaintive song. He could hear some of the words. It was a sad song, sung deep-throated. That would be Marie Shannon, the woman on the billboard out front. She sang well. She knew which songs to sing to the men who flocked to the Golden Bull to hear her. Mostly miners, some cowboys, a few hard-cases. She sang of an old flame, a lost love, and the wounds carried in a girl's heart.

Morgan stepped out of the shadows, mingled with the sparse remnants of the crowd. A few men went inside. Morgan stepped with them, as if he was one of their party. Someone shushed them when they walked in, and Morgan slid along the wall to look over the crowd at the bar, at the tables and, like himself, leaning against the wall, rapt looks on their faces.

Marie Shannon finished the song. Tumultuous applause broke out in the room. Men stood and cheered. Someone threw cut flowers onto the stage. Marie picked up the bouquet, bowed graciously, and blew a kiss to the cheering audience. Morgan found himself applauding with the rest.

There was something vaguely familiar about her. But he couldn't put his finger on it.

The curtains closed and the orchestra went into a lively dance number.

Morgan froze as someone grabbed his elbow, squeezed.

He turned, his hand floating above the butt of his pistol, looked into the eyes of Rudy Owens.

"Hello, Mister Morgan. Thought that was you. You cut off your beard."

"Jesus, kid," Morgan said tightly. "Don't do that too often."

Rudy's hand floated away from Morgan's elbow, an awkward appendage at the end of his arm.

"Sorry, Mister Morgan. But I got to talk to you. It's real important. I mean, Mister Anvic."

Morgan cracked a wry smile. "Anvic or Morgan. It's all the same. The cat's out of the bag now. What's on your mind, Rudy?"

Owens looked around furtively. His hands shook. Morgan looked at him, puzzled. Something had spooked the lad.

"Come on, I'll buy you a drink," Morgan said, heading for the bar.

Morgan found an open place at the far end. There was a hallway leading to the back and a closed door marked Office.

"Whiskey?" he asked Rudy.

Owens nodded.

"Whiskey," Morgan told the bartender, whose shirt was dripping with sweat. His apron was begrimed, and it was plain that he had been busy all evening like the other two men serving drinks.

Rudy's hand shook when he picked up the glass, drank the whiskey.

Morgan sipped slowly, his eyes flickering as he looked over the crowd before taking up an interest in Rudy Owens again.

"Go ahead, Rudy, get it off your chest."

"Well, sir," Rudy whispered, "you know when I saw

176

you at Russ House you said you didn't . . . didn't do what they say you did and you said someone else did."

"Yeah. A man named Trask. Luke Trask."

Rudy's face blanched. His eyes blinked. "Trask! I wondered. I'm no dummy, Mister Morgan. I can put two and two together and come up with four."

"You know Trask?" Morgan leaned on the bar with his elbows, drew closer to Rudy.

"Don't know him except by sight. But I been thinkin' a lot since me and Curly come in from Fort Huachuca. He was acting mighty peculiar and just turned on me real quick after we come to Tombstone. Then I seed him with this Trask. I seen 'em both together a lot lately. And Curly, he don't like to look me in the eye no more."

Morgan's jaw hardened. A muscle twitched along the bone. "Curly and Trask?" he said.

Rudy nodded.

"Go on," Morgan said.

"What you said right now, that Trask done it. Killed your family. That made my stomach turn over. Curly's always talkin' big about bein' hooked up with Ringo or someone and now he's with Trask. And . . . he's got plenty of money, but he don't work. So, I figure he told Trask you was going to be gone that day, the day it happened."

Morgan's eyes burned a hard blue.

What Rudy had said made sense. Someone would have had to tell Trask where he ranched, that he would be gone the day Bonnie, Tommy, and Pedro were killed. His thoughts went back to that time. Curly had asked a lot of questions. And, two days before they'd made the drive to Fort Huachuca, he had sent Curly

177

in to Benson for supplies. Curly had volunteered. Yet the man had pretended to be his friend. He appeared to be honest.

"Are you sure about Curly and Trask?" Morgan asked.

"They was just in here a while ago. And that other man, too. Parsons."

"Parsons here?"

"He left before Curly got here. Then there was that shooting. I saw the marshal trying to catch that girl, chase her out of here. We heard two blasts from a shotgun and next thing I know there's a dead marshal. Curly and Trask sat there the whole time. Everybody else rushed out to see what was going on, me included, but those two didn't get up until later."

"Where'd they go?"

"I saw Curly leave. I don't know where that Trask went."

Morgan's eyes swept the room again.

"Mister Morgan, that ain't all. I seen Trask talkin' to a lawman a few times. This lawman is the one spreadin' the word about you bein' a murderer and he asks questions in ever place I go. Shows them fliers with your face on it."

"The lawman got a name?"

"Harris. Delbert Harris. He's new in town, they say."

Morgan looked at Rudy Owens with new respect. He put an arm on the youth's shoulder. "Rudy, thanks. You've done me a favor. I'm mighty grateful."

"Was I you, Mister Morgan, I'd lay low. You got too many men hunting you."

"You know where I am, Rudy. If you run into Curly, or Trask, or Parsons, come and get me. Fast."

Morgan patted him on the back.

Rudy smiled. "I surely will, Mister Morgan," he said, a little too loud.

Someone coughed behind Morgan's back. He turned, looked into the face of a short, wizened man with a swamper's broom in his hands, an apron wrapped around faded trousers.

"You," the swamper said to Morgan, "please to come with me. Miss Shannon wants to see you."

"Who, me?" Morgan pointed a finger at his chest.

"Just you," the swamper said, frowning at Rudy Owens.

"You go on," Rudy said. "I've got to get some shut-eye. Those mines open up awful early in the mornin'."

Morgan paid for the drinks, followed the man with the broom to the door marked Office.

"I'm Wilbur Pratt," the little man said, tapping politely on the office door. "I work for Miss Shannon, personal." He talked with a slight impediment. He was typical of men who had fought in the War Between the States and had come out of it without any visible wounds. The noise of battle, the fear, the carnage, had taken something out of them. Such men usually wound up on the public dole or in menial jobs.

"Come in," a woman's voice said.

Wilbur opened the door. "Here he is, Miss Shannon," said Pratt. "Chad Morgan."

"Thank you, Wilbur," Marie Shannon said, rising from behind her desk. "That will be all for now."

"Yes'm. I'll be right outside, case you need me."

Morgan suppressed a smile. It seemed that Wilbur fancied himself the lady's protector and champion.

The door closed behind him and Morgan could hear Wilbur's wheezing breath just beyond it. He took a step forward.

Marie Shannon was even more beautiful close up. Her long blonde hair was natural now, the sequins having been removed. She wore a green velvet robe, open at the throat. Melonlike breasts protruded partially. Morgan gathered she wore nothing but the dressing robe, since it clung to her shapely form so tightly.

"So you're Chad Morgan," she said, sitting on the edge of her desk. The robe fell away from her legs.

Morgan tried to focus on her nut-brown eyes, but the legs dangled tantalizingly over the edge of the desk.

"Maybe," Morgan said. "I go by the name of Anvic. F.B. Anvic."

Marie laughed. A tinkling array of musical notes. Her laugh was infectious.

Morgan only smiled.

"I won't call you Anvic. Wilbur tells me what goes on out there. He heard another man call you Morgan. And I've seen your picture often enough. The mustache won't hide you for long."

"What's the point, Miss Shannon?"

"You don't remember me at all, do you?" There was a bitter edge to her tone. "Funny. I thought of you and wondered how it would be when we met again. I imagined that you would take me in your arms and smother me with kisses and tell me how you yearned for me all these years."

Morgan looked at her sharply, trying to understand her meaning. He looked around the office, as if trying to find some clue as to why he ought to know her. The flowers that had been thrown up onstage were in a vase. The desk had a quill pen standing next to an inkwell, a few papers scattered on it, an ashtray full of frayed matchsticks and a cigar butt, a paperweight. The walls had a few prints. Currier & Ives, a photograph or two. Both of these were blurred, faded. Billboard posters adorned two of the walls, both featuring Marie Shannon.

Shannon. The name was familiar. Marie was not at all familiar. He would remember a name like that.

"I'm sorry, ma'am. I never knew anybody named Marie. And the only Shannon I know of is clear back in—"

"Ellsworth. Paul Shannon? He's dead, I'm sorry to say."

"Paul Shannon? Yeah. I worked for him once. I was just a kid. That was back in Ellsworth. You kin to him?"

"I'm his daughter," Marie said flatly. Her disappointment showed in the dour expression on her face. "Bonnie Lewis and I used to be close friends until she met you. After that I didn't see her much anymore. You went to work for Taylor at the freight office."

Recognition slowly crept into Morgan's consciousness. "You're Myrtle!" he said, grinning.

Marie shuddered. "A name I loathe! I changed it to Marie. For professional reasons."

"How did you come to own this place?"

"Pa came here, struck it rich in silver. Bought the building. Mainly to give me a chance to be what I wanted to be. A singer. He died two years ago and—"

"I'm sorry, Myrtle . . . Marie."

"I didn't bring you here to talk about myself," she said, sliding off the desk. She came close to him, appraised him with frank brown eyes. He smelled the heady scent of her perfume, the talc, the womanly musk of her. "It's Bonnie. They say you murdered her and you had a little boy, too."

"I didn't murder anyone."

She let out a sigh. "I believe you," she said. "Even before you walked in here. Unfortunately, a man was killed outside my place tonight and that man was holding a warrant for your arrest. They're saying you shot him because you're on the run."

Morgan said nothing. A warning bell was tolling in some subterranean cavern of his brain. A sunken chime that was faint and faraway.

"All right," she said abruptly, turning away. "It's my turn to say I'm sorry. About Bonnie. And your son. I was jealous of her a long time ago. You fought over her. Killed Ned Trask!"

"You knew him. He was a hothead. He came after me. I won't apologize for that. But it wasn't murder."

The bell got louder.

"Will you let me help you, Chad? I live in the Harwood house on Fremont. I bought it from Bill after that shoot-out at the O.K. Corral two years ago. After Billy Clanton died there, Bill didn't want to live there anymore."

"I know it."

"Come see me. Tonight, if you want. I have one more short show to do and then—"

"Some other time. Do you know why I came here?"

"No. It wasn't a very smart thing to do."

"I'm hunting Luke Trask. He killed Bonnie. He and

three other men. One of them is dead. The others are here in Tombstone, I'm sure. Trask and Parsons were here tonight."

"Oh? I haven't seen Luke in years."

The bell clanged.

Marie Shannon was lying. He knew she was. But why?

"I'll be going now, Marie. I wish you every success."

She stiffened, then relaxed.

"Please think about my offer. I . . . I'd love to see you in private. Talk over old times."

"Maybe I will stop in," he said lamely.

"It's funny how things work out, isn't it?"

"What do you mean?"

"If I had married you, instead of Bonnie, I might be the one lying in a grave now."

He didn't answer. He opened the door. Wilbur Pratt almost fell into the room. Morgan turned, raised a hand. "Good-bye, Marie," he said.

His eyes went to the ashtray again. Something about those matchsticks bothered him. Triggered a trace of memory. It was there, just out of reach, crawling up the walls of his mind. Something important. Something he had seen somewhere before and couldn't recall for certain.

"I'll be seeing you, Chad," Marie said as he walked away. "Real soon."

CHAPTER TWENTY

Morgan saw no sign of anyone watching Russ House when he returned. He tiptoed past Gabriela's room and opened the door to his own room quietly. Inside, he locked the door and felt his way to the bed. He did not light the lamp. Gabriela had asked him to stop in when he returned, but he was weary and strangely keyed up. Carmen, he realized, had made the bed before she left.

It had been awkward with the two women there. Gabriela's accusing eyes, Carmen's embarrassment, his own.

He had wanted to ask Gabriela about Lucinda, but that could wait.

He was getting close. Parsons had murdered the marshal, Barker, and that told him something. He did Trask's dirty work for him.

And Jack Curly Garth—he would have to be added to the list. If he had told Trask about the drive to Fort Huachuca, then he was as much responsible for the deaths on the ranch as Luke Trask.

Where would it stop? How would it end?

He slipped off his boots, undressed in the dark. He hung his gunbelt over the bedstead and crawled under the covers. Weariness rolled over him. He threw an arm up over his forehead, stared into the dark.

Marie Shannon. Little Myrtle Shannon, daughter of Paul Shannon, who used to run cattle on a little spread outside of Ellsworth. Now she was the owner of a saloon in the roughest town north of the border. A woman scorned. He had never known until now. He had been so smitten with Bonnie that he'd hardly noticed anyone else.

So what was he doing now? Making up for lost time?

Morgan turned over on his stomach, shut his eyes. He felt the faint tugs of pain from the all-but-forgotten wounds.

He let the sleep come. Let it overtake him like a warm sea tide floating him to a peaceful shore, safe harbor.

José Mendoza did not recognize the man in the blanket poncho, the *serape*, at first.

"*Buenos días,*" Morgan grinned. He wore a flat-crowned Stetson, wide-brimmed, with a leather thong tied under his chin.

"It is you, Morgan! And you come to the back door like a servant. *Por qué?*"

"I'll walk out the front door if you have what I asked for. I think I lost my shadow about two blocks away."

"You were followed?"

"From the moment I left the hotel."

"*Aii, qué lástima!* A friend has to sneak around to

see me. And my ears are ringing with the chatter of my daughter. She glows, Morgan, she shines."

"I will say hello to Carmen when we have finished our business."

José limped away from the chair, where he sat on the back porch. He had been polishing brass pots with pumice and water, cleaning out the *olla* to make fresh *tepache*. The wooden stump left pockmarks in the dirt. He walked to a small shed on the other side of the building, opened the door. "In there," he said. "I hope it is right."

Morgan stepped around him, adjusting his eyes to the dimness. There, stacked against the wall, was what he was looking for. He picked it up, hefted it, checked the leather straps. They were strong enough. The two large chest-size pieces of iron were connected by the leather straps, sewn together with thick strips of raw-hide. The outfit was heavy. He set the iron down, took off his hat. Morgan slipped the poncho over his head, put on the sandwich-board vest. Then he put the poncho on over it.

José looked on in amazement.

"The bullet-proof vest, no?"

"I hope it'll slow 'em down. The men I'm after like to shoot from ambush. If they go for the head, I'm out of luck. I'm hoping they'll shoot me in the back or try for the heart."

José shuddered.

Shafts of sunlight filtered through the shed. Morgan put his hat back on, squared it on his head. He walked around in a small circle. He was packing at least thirty extra pounds, but the straps were wide enough not to dig into his shoulder blades. The open sides of the poncho allowed his arms and hands freedom of movement. He made a quick draw.

José hobbled backward, startled. "Fast," the Mexican said.

"Let's hope fast enough."

It was past noon. Morgan had slept late, managed to leave the hotel without running into Gabriela. He'd eaten steak and beans for breakfast at a small café on Allen Street after shaking the man following him. Twenty minutes after leaving the Grub Steak, he had seen his shadow again. The man was careless, stupid. Followed him over to Allen, a block behind. He didn't stop the man, because he knew who he was, where to find him.

"I will see Carmen later," Morgan told José. "Tell her I said howdy."

"She will be disappointed."

"So will I, José."

The mine whistles blew as Morgan walked down Allen toward the Golden Bull. One o'clock. Their echoes died out over the flatlands, rang hauntingly in the low hills.

A block from the Golden Bull, Morgan saw the man who had been following him. It was obvious that he had been combing the street, looking for his lost prey. Morgan stifled the urge to laugh. The man was still looking and he had no idea he was now being followed himself.

Wilbur Pratt went inside M. Calisher & Son's store. He had just left the Nevada Boot & Shoe Store that featured "Gents Furnishing Goods." By day, Allen Street was a thriving commercial center. It was only at night that its red railroad lanterns were lit and the painted hurdy-gurdy gals plied their wares in the cantinas, the cribs, the saloons and gambling halls that were tucked in between the mercantile stores, lumber companies, and restaurants.

Morgan waited for him in the shade of the shingled roof next door. He leaned against a square-cut post under the eaves, building a quirly. He lit it and felt the smoke scratch at his throat, bite into his lungs.

Pratt, in dark duster and battered felt hat, came out of Calisher's and hurried to the establishment next door.

Morgan fell in step beside him.

The little man looked up, his face drained of blood.

"Just keep on walking, Pratt," Morgan said. "One wrong move and I'll wring your neck like a chicken."

"Yes, sir," Pratt gasped.

"Why are you following me?"

"Wanted to tell you somethin'," he stammered. "I . . . I didn't mean no harm, honest."

"Spill it." Morgan rubbed against Pratt's arm, kept him close to the buildings on that side of the street, in the shade. People passing by paid no notice of the two men.

"Heard Parsons talking to a couple of men last night after you went back to the hotel. Nobody pays me much mind. I hear a lot."

"Yeah, Pratt. I bet you do. Now what's this about Parsons?"

"You know Buster Tate? Angus Kyle?"

"No."

"They're right handy with six-guns, Mister Morgan. In fact, that's their trade. Parsons, he wants to set you up, have those two at your back."

188

"Why are you telling me this?"

"I know you and Miss Shannon are old friends. I keep my ears open. I like Miss Shannon. She treats me decent. Parsons means to brace you at the Golden Bull. He's over there now, I reckon, and those other two men are right close. I followed you to Russ House last night. When I come back to the Golden Bull they was there settin' it all up."

"Marie know you're telling me this?" Morgan stopped and looked at Pratt's pinched face as he stopped the man with a hand on his arm.

Pratt shook his head.

"All right, Pratt. Tell me where these two randies are, what they look like."

"Parsons will be sitting in the center of the room, alone. Tate and Kyle will be settin' near the front doors, on both sides. They're going to shoot you in the back, mister. You don't stand a chance if'n you go in there."

Morgan smiled. He tossed his cigarette down, then reached under his poncho, fumbled in his shirt pocket. His hand came out holding a wad of cotton. He broke the wad into two pieces.

"How do they know I'll be at the Golden Bull?"

"They don't. They was going to wait there ever' afternoon till you showed up."

Morgan stuffed cotton into one ear, then the other.

"Why didn't you just come up and tell me about Parsons this morning?"

"Was going to, but lost you."

Morgan smiled.

"I figured you might go on back to the Golden Bull and I'd find you there. You'll be a dead man if you walk in there."

Morgan patted the man patronizingly on the shoulder. "I'm going there now, friend. You go on back there and get out of the way. You tell Parsons I'm coming. I want him to know. I want him to sweat it."

Pratt's face paled once again. "What will I say? He'll know I told you he—"

"Just tell everyone there that a man's hunting Parsons and you saw him. Tell them the man's name is Chad Morgan."

Pratt swallowed hard. His eyes watered. He thought it over, nodded quickly.

Morgan waited, watched Wilbur Pratt waddle into the Golden Bull. He waited five minutes, then walked slowly across the street on an angle.

He pushed through the batwing doors, stood there for a moment, his eyes adjusting to the light.

It was quiet inside. Like a tomb.

Wilbur Pratt stood, white-faced, at the far end of the bar. The barkeep's hand stopped in midair as he reached for a glass. Three or four men stood at the bar, staring at the poncho-clad man who had just entered.

In the center of the room, Fred Parsons sat, facing the batwing doors.

On the table, a sawed-off shotgun lay within easy reach. It was cocked. Fred's hands lay flat on the tabletop.

Morgan glanced around the room.

A man sat on his right in a chair near the wall. The chair leaned against the wall, but the man's feet were firmly planted on the floor. He wore a thin mustache, a battered hat crimped to a peak. His pistol was tied low on his leg. His hand was less than six inches away from the butt.

Another man, on his left, leaned against the wall near the door. He was tall, lean, wore a sombrero. His pistol, too, was tied down, ran from his thigh to his knee. His hand floated near the butt of his plow-handle. His face bristled with a three-day beard.

Morgan took a step toward Fred Parsons. His boots crunched grit under the soles and heels on the hardwood floor.

A man at the bar cleared his throat.

Parsons stared at him steady.

Neither of the men by the wall moved.

A glass tinkled as someone moved an arm on the bar.

Morgan took another step toward Parsons. His *serape* whispered against his legs. His arms hung outside, hands visible.

Parsons didn't move.

Morgan stood twenty paces away. "Go for it, Parsons," he said, crouching.

Parsons moved his hands like a card player reaching for chips.

Morgan's right hand was a shadow—a bird's shadow streaking, a diving hawk's shadow. He filled his hand, hammered back. The pistol bucked in his hand as Parsons picked up the double-barreled scattergun.

Behind him, motion, sound.

His slug burst the flesh in the center of Parsons's chest.

Parsons's hands twitched and the shotgun clattered onto the table. He half rose, his face contorted with pain. His hand clawed for his pistol as a blood rose spread across his chest. He drew, somehow, fired pointblank at Morgan.

A puff of dust rose off the *serape*. Morgan jerked with the hard flat pain that crushed his chest.

Two shots boomed behind him.

Sledgehammers clanged into his back, slammed the iron plate against his spine.

Parsons fell across the table, a fist-size hole in his back. Spreading like red oil on the table, blood pumped over the shotgun. He slid down, eyes frosted with the glaze of death.

Morgan staggered and fanned the hammer back on his .44 Remington.

Pain blurred his vision, buckled his knees.

Through the haze of agonizing shoots of pain, he fired at the man closest to him.

Buster Tate uttered a short scream as the lead ball ripped into his gut, two inches above his belt buckle.

Angus Kyle fired at Morgan again.

The bullet struck the breastplate, putting a clean hole through the *serape*. Morgan shot backward. One knee buckled. With a mighty effort, he thumbed back his hammer, took aim at Angus Kyle. Searing pain shot across his chest, burrowed deep into the ribs, the muscles. He squeezed the trigger as Kyle stepped forward.

Angus Kyle twisted as the bullet drummed into his heart, bursting it like a muskmelon. He danced sideways on rubbery legs, blood pumping in jetting spurts from the hole in his chest.

He crashed to the floor in a bloody heap.

Buster Tate twitched once, against the wall. One hand clutched the hole in his belly. He glared at Morgan with steely, glittering eyes. He opened his mouth, but no sound came out.

Morgan walked over, kicked his legs out from under him.

Buster crashed forward onto his face. A widening stain of blood spread from him. He groaned in agony.

Morgan stepped over him, smoke curling from the barrel of his pistol.

He walked through the batwing doors, standing straight and tall. His chest burned with fire. His breath came hard.

Behind him, men's voices rose in wonder.

Morgan ignored them. He walked down the center of the street toward Fifth. He ejected empty shells, crammed in fresh ones. He holstered his pistol, shook off the pain. His jaw was set tight, though, and his blue eyes sparkled with light.

He wondered if he could make it to Russ House without falling down.

Despite the cotton in his ears, they buzzed with the echoes of the terrible explosions.

Men stared at him, but no one made a move to stop him.

Instead, they shrank away, afraid of the man in the bullet-torn poncho—a man, who by all that was right, ought to be lying dead in a pool of his own blood.

CHAPTER TWENTY-ONE

Chad Morgan walked up the stairs to his room. The desk clerk craned his neck to stare. Whispers drifted up from the lobby. At his door, Morgan started to collapse.

His legs gave way. Sweat broke out on his forehead. A wave of dizziness assailed him as he struggled to put the key in the lock. The door wavered and his vision clouded. He got the key in, leaned against the door for support. He turned the key with effort. The door opened.

Morgan staggered inside, kicking the door shut.

There was no energy left to lock it.

He fell into a chair, panted for breath.

Pinpoints of pain throbbed in his ribs, in the muscles of his back, in his spine. It felt as if someone had taken a hammer and pounded nails into his flesh, his bones. He shrugged out of the poncho, hefted the bullet-resistant vest from his shoulders. It clanged to the floor. He peeled out of his shirt and touched the painful spots, where the bullets had spanged the vest. He looked at the heavy iron vest, saw the lead smudges where he had taken the hits.

The door opened quietly.

Morgan reacted. His hand flew instinctively to his pistol, grasped the butt.

"Chad Morgan? It is me, Gabriela Gomez."

He saw her then, as she stepped cautiously inside. She was panting for breath.

"Oh, it's you," he groaned.

"What happened?"

Morgan had left the key in the lock on the outside of the door. Gabriela removed it, shut the door, locked it. She stood there, shaking.

"I hurt," he said, struggling to his feet. He towered over her.

"Can I help?" Her breathing was labored.

"No." He felt his chest and winced when he touched a tender spot. "There's nothing broken. Just badly bruised."

Her eyes looked in puzzlement at the iron plate on the floor, the red welts on his chest.

"You were shot." It was a flat statement.

"Sort of," he grinned. He walked gingerly to the bed, crawled atop the covers. Gabriela came over, handed him his key. He tossed it on the bedside table.

"Won't you tell me what happened?" she asked. "I care. You look pale as wax."

Haltingly, he told her what had happened, every heave of his chest a sharp pain through his torso. The vest had absorbed most of the energy of the bullets, but the bruises went deep, he knew. The pain was fierce. For the first time, Morgan noticed that Gabriela was as pale as he was. Her features were drawn, her

195

lips trembling. She listened, then put her face in her hands. She began sobbing.

"What's the matter?" he asked, reaching out to touch her arm.

She sat on the bed next to him. She smelled of olives and garlic, of fresh-ground cornmeal and baking tortillas, of red wine and desert flowers.

"I heard that you were killed," she said. "Chad, I . . . I thought you were dead. I rushed over here and the people downstairs looked as if they had seen a ghost. Everyone said you were shot several times. Now I know why they acted so strange when you just walked out of that saloon and down the street."

"I'm alive. Thanks to that iron vest over there. But I can't stay here. Once Trask figures it out, he'll be bracing me. I want to face him on my own terms, not his."

"Come to my room," she said. "You will be safer there. I have some balm that will soothe your hurts."

Morgan thought about it a minute.

Gabriela wasted no time. She swooped up his shirt in her hand, helped him up.

Morgan groaned with pain as he picked up his rifle. Gabriela hurried him down the hall to her room. Inside, she locked the door. "Lie down on my bed," she ordered.

Morgan eased down to the bed, stretched out, as Gabriela slid a table over next to the bed. On it were jars of unguents and balms.

"Turn over," she said.

He rolled over carefully so that he lay flat on his stomach. Delicate but strong hands applied a soothing balm to his back. She turned him over on his back and did the same to his chest. He felt the heat soak into his flesh.

"Did you learn this in the convent?" he said in a teasing manner as he began to relax.

"No," she said. "I was never in a convent. And Pedro was not my father. I was a concubine."

"What?" Morgan was stunned. "But Tío Pedro thought . . . He said—"

"Tío Pedro killed my father."

Morgan couldn't believe what he was hearing. "Not Pedro. He wouldn't kill anybody."

"My father was a most cruel man, deserving of death. Pedro adopted me, felt responsible. He put me in a convent, but I paid my way out, bribed the sisters to handle my mail. My own father raped me, Morgan. Pedro killed him. Pedro was my uncle."

"And all the time—"

"Yes. I did not want to break his heart, but I was not made to live in a convent. I lived with a most generous man. A man who taught me many things. Now, be still, Chad Morgan. You must sleep. No one will bother you here."

"What will you do?"

"I will watch over you. I will be your ears, your eyes." Gabriela stroked his forehead as she spoke.

Relaxed, Morgan closed his eyes and fell asleep before the thoughts of the recent violence could crowd into his thoughts.

Morgan woke with a start.
The world was shaking, pounding.
The room was dark.

"Quickly. Put your shirt on," Gabriela whispered. "They know you are here."

Groggily, Morgan sat up, eased out of bed. Gabriela handed him his shirt, then picked up a small nickel-plated pistol, a .32 Smith & Wesson. "Who is it?" she called.

"Open up. I'm Deputy Harris. I have a warrant for the arrest of Chad Morgan. We know he's in there."

Morgan strapped on his pistol.

"Go away!" Gabriela shouted. "I'm alone!"

"Bullshit, lady. I'll shoot my way in if I have to."

Morgan was ready.

"No," Gabriela whispered. "You must get away. The window!"

Morgan walked over to it. He lifted the shade, looked out onto Fifth Street. The lower roof was just beneath the window. He could jump there, slide down. The drop would be about a dozen feet or so. He could make it.

"Open up or I start shooting this door apart!" Harris shouted.

"Go!" Gabriela whispered.

"I'll be at El Tecolote, at the end of Allen Street," Morgan told her.

"I know it," she said. "Hurry."

Morgan was halfway out the window when the shots rang out. He hesitated.

Gabriela rushed up and pushed him the rest of the way out. His boots hit the slanting roof. He fell on his rump, started sliding. He reached out to grab something, but nothing was there. He went over the edge, dropped to the street in darkness.

It was deserted.
Above him, more shots.
Two of them—at least two—were small caliber.

CHAPTER TWENTY-TWO

"It looks very bad for you, *amigo*," José Mendoza said. "Sheriff Rushmore's men are combing the town for you."

Morgan's blue eyes dulled with the shadows of memory. It was morning and he had spent a fitful night in José's house. Worrying. Now his fears were confirmed.

"You're telling me that Gabriela Gomez is dead and that they are saying I killed her?"

José nodded solemnly. He sat one-legged on the kitchen chair, his wooden leg unstrapped, leaning against the table. Carmen sat stiffly next to Morgan, her eyes wet.

"That can't be true!" she said.

"Who is saying this?" Morgan asked.

"A deputy named Delbert Harris. He has a Winchester rifle that is yours. He is saying that you shot the girl with that rifle."

"Harris is a liar," Morgan said. "You know him?"

"He is new."

"Describe him for me."

"He is a nervous man. He has the light hair that comes to his shoulders. His lips are thin, narrow. He is a young man with pale eyes. He has the spit at the corners of his mouth all the time, as if he is rabid."

Morgan closed his eyes. He heard Bonnie's voice again, describing those who raped her. Describing the man who roped little Tommy, dragged him.

"Anything else?" he said, opening his eyes.

"On his hand he has the tattoo. The initials of his name. D.H."

"Delbert Harris," Morgan mused. "Or Dave Higgins."

"What do you mean?" asked José.

Morgan got up from the table, paced the floor as José and his daughter stared at him. "It has to be him. He claims I killed Gabriela. He knows I didn't. He's been dogging my heels. Everywhere I turn, his damned name comes up. José, I need some favors. It's important, but it could be dangerous."

"Anything you ask, my friend."

Morgan sat back down, leaned over the table. He spoke earnestly. "There is a man who works for Marie Shannon at the Golden Bull. Wilbur Pratt. Get a message to him. Tell him I want to talk to Marie. Here. Day after tomorrow. Eight o'clock in the evening. Sharp. Don't tell Marie direct. And don't let Pratt tell her you gave him the message. Tell him it's important I talk to her. A matter of life and death."

"I will do this. He is the swamper there. I know his face."

"Good. Then I want you to see this Deputy Delbert Harris. Tell him you want to buy a piece of jewelry. A wedding ring with a small diamond. Tell him you will

201

pay in gold. If he does not have the ring, then follow him. See where he goes."

"This ring, you know of it?"

"It was Bonnie's wedding ring. Either Harris, if that's his name, or Luke Trask, must have it. Either way, if Harris meets Trask, I'll know. Be careful. If he does have it, there will be one more thing you will have to do. I will tell you what I will need once this Harris takes the baited hook. *Ten cuidado, amigo mío.*"

"Do not worry. I will be your eyes and your ears."

Morgan grimaced. Those were the same words Gabriela had used. And now she was dead.

Spittle bubbled at the corners of Deputy Sheriff Delbert Harris's mouth. He blew and sucked at the bubbles until they expanded and contracted. His pale-blue eyes were vacuous.

"You've cinched it, all right," Trask said, "but around a damned empty barrel. You let the bastard get away."

"Hell, it was that woman what helped him, Trask. She singed my hairs with that little nickel-plated widowmaker so's I had to cut her down, cover my tracks."

"So now the reward for Morgan has gone up and he's still free. Christ, Parsons had him cold."

"What about Kyle and Tate?"

"Who'd have thought the bastard would wear an iron vest? He's some sneaky sonofabitch."

"Sneakier'n you think," Harris said, picking up a shredded match that Trask had discarded. They sat in the Lone Wolf, drinking from a pail of Zang's. Trask looked like hell, Harris thought. The man's eyes were red-rimmed, his face bloated from drink. He chewed matches one after the other. Well, he had a lot on his mind.

"What's that supposed to mean?" Trask snarled, cocking his head back as he glared at the erstwhile deputy.

"Had a visitor a few minutes ago, up at the Golden Bull. He wanted to buy a wedding ring."

"Yeah?" Trask still hadn't gotten it.

Harris played him on out with the mental rope, like a calf running with the slack. He'd get jerked when he got to the end of the riata.

"Wanted a particular ring. Small diamond, gold. 'Bout like that one you took off'n Morgan's woman."

Trask exploded in a rage. He shot a hand across the table, grabbed Harris's vest, twisted it in his fist.

"Who, dammit? Who asked you?"

"Don't know. A Mexican. I seen him around."

"You asshole. He's in with Morgan." Trask's teeth ground down on the matchstick in his mouth, splintered it.

"Back off, Luke. Curly's follerin' the Mexican. He should be back anytime to let me know who he is, where he is. I figger he'll lead us right smack to Morgan."

Trask relaxed his fingers, released his grip on Harris's vest. Harris seemed unruffled, sure of himself.

Trask had changed. He was no longer the cocksure leader he had been. Harris didn't know what had changed him, but he had a few ideas. Morgan's killing of Parsons was part of it. But, he suspected, Trask had another reason for being nervous. He had himself a woman. Harris didn't know who she was yet, but all the signs were there. Trask was short-tempered, nervous, half-asleep in the day, bright-eyed at night. He had shaved off his rough beard, taking to wearing toilet water. He had bought new clothes, kept his boots shined.

"You and I are the only ones left of the old bunch," Trask said sourly. He extracted pieces of matchstick from his teeth, took a swallow of beer. He rinsed out his mouth with the brew, spat splinters of wood on the floor. "Curly ain't one of us. In time, he could work out, but he's still green."

"I know. Morgan's a thorn in your side. We need to get back to work. I can't stomach Henry Rushmore much damned longer."

"You stay clear of Morgan, Dave," Trask said, forgetting that Dave Higgins was now Delbert Harris. "Just get a line on him and let me take the bastard out. I shoulda done that when we rubbed out his woman and kid."

"Revenge is a funny thing," Harris mused. "Like a two-edged Bowie. You grab it wrong and it can cut you to pieces."

"Don't give me no bunkhouse philosophy, dammit."

The men were interrupted by a shadow in the doorway. Curly Garth came inside the saloon, sweating profusely. He stalked straight to their table.

"Well?" Trask asked.

Curly Garth sat down, pushed his hat back off his bald head. His pate was slick with sweat.

"I follered that Mexican. He went straight to the Golden Bull after he left you, Delbert."

"Huh?" Harris said.

"He braced Wilbur Pratt, said something to him.

Wilbur went straight into Miss Shannon's office, blathered something. I follered the Mex." Curly grinned wide. "He owns a little cantina called El Tecolote on the end of Allen. And that's where Morgan's holed up. I walked around back to the house part and heard Chad Morgan jawin' with a Mexican gal, the one-legged Mex's daughter."

"Sonofabitch!" Trask exclaimed. "You done good, Curly."

"And that ain't all, Trask," Curly smiled. "I went back and worked over Wilbur Pratt pretty good. Found out what the Mex told him."

Curly paused. Trask leaned forward. Harris eyed him with pale doll's eyes, empty as buttons.

"Get to it, Curly," Trask growled low.

"Morgan wants Miss Shannon to meet him at El Tecolote day after tomorrow."

Trask's eyes blazed. His jaw tightened. The veins in his neck stood out in silent rage.

Suddenly, Harris had the answer to one of his questions about Trask.

He was sweet on Marie Shannon.

And it looked like Morgan was making a play for her.

Delbert Harris shivered in the chill night air.

His horse stomped the ground impatiently. The animal, a Roman-nosed bay, did not belong to him, but he had good bottom, sound chest, strong legs. He was one of Trask's string. Trask did not know Harris was riding that particular horse.

Harris didn't care. Luke Trask had lost his punch,

and Harris was tired of taking his orders, jumping every time Trask snapped his fingers. He was loco over the saloon singer and hadn't planned a robbery. And that damned Morgan had him buffaloed. Well, no more. Even if Trask had said to keep an eye on Morgan, not to kill him, he didn't have to take his orders. He wore the badge. He was in the clear. Besides, there was a way to kill two birds with one chunk of rock.

The lights in El Tecolote winked out across the street.

Harris rode out of the shadows, the horse's hooves muffled in the thick dust of the wide street.

The Mexican had offered gold for the wedding ring. Morgan was back there, hiding out.

He could kill them both, pocket the gold, and move up a notch in Rushmore's eyes, the town's. Chad Morgan was a wanted man. Trask had no claim on him. Not anymore. He had slowed down, was moon-eyed over Marie Shannon. He was old.

An hour ago the Mexican had brought a horse in from the livery, tied it out back. Morgan's horse, Harris reckoned. The man was getting ready to light a shuck. The horse was a big black gelding, sixteen hands high, at least. Four white stockings. The kind of horse a man like Morgan would ride. Well, he wouldn't be needing it anymore. Not after Harris did what he had come to do.

He rode between two buildings two doors down from El Tecolote, through the shadows, into the back alley dusted with moonlight. Lamps glowed through the windows of the house in back of the cantina, burnished them to an orange-gold sheen. The coal-black gelding stood under a shed, saddled. The horse whinnied softly.

Harris smiled.

The back door opened.

José Mendoza stepped out, looked in the direction of Morgan's horse.

Harris dug spurs into the blunt-nosed bay, drew his pistol.

"*Quién es?*" José called out. "Who is there?"

Harris raised his arm, cocked the pistol, took aim. The hammer made a noise as it engaged the sear. José looked in the direction of the sound, eyes wide.

"Who's out there?" he asked in English. "Is that you, Deputy Harris?"

Harris cursed. José Mendoza quickly stepped back inside the doorway. The deputy let his gun arm fall. Something was wrong. He looked around him at the deep shadows, the mass of buildings that now seemed threatening. The lamps in the Mendoza house went out all at once. The alley was plunged into an eerie silence.

"Higgins?" a soft voice called behind him.

Harris wheeled, swinging his gun arm.

Something whispered toward him, out of the dark. He heard it hiss, like a snake. A shadowy snake leaped out of the dark. He threw up his arms. His finger squeezed the trigger. The bullet whined off into the night.

The lariat dropped over Harris's shoulders, jerked tight.

"No!" he screamed.

The rope hauled tight, pinning his arms. The pistol dropped from his hand, thunked into the dust. Glittered in the moonlight.

Chad Morgan jerked the rope tight, jerked it hard.

"How's it feel, Higgins?" he said, as Higgins flew out of the saddle.

Higgins hit the ground like a sack of meal. His senses jarred on impact.

Morgan ran for Captain Joe, looped the rope around the saddle horn, pulled himself up. He leaned over, grasped the reins with one hand. Captain Joe took out the slack, sidling sideways, like the trained cowhorse he was. Morgan dug his spurs into the animal's flanks, reined him toward the open space at the edge of Tombstone.

Higgins screamed as his body was jerked like a puppet on the end of the rope.

Morgan felt the weight hit the end of the rope. Captain Joe dug in, gathered speed. Higgins's horse shied, galloped off in the opposite direction. Lamps came on in the Mendoza house once again. The back door opened. José, Carmen, and Sheriff Henry Rushmore stepped outside.

"Be right back!" Morgan shouted.

Higgins screamed again as his body bounced, twisted, then stretched out straight as Captain Joe gathered speed.

Morgan rode straight into the open country. He pulled Higgins through Spanish bayonets, over rocks, through gritty dust. He looked back over his shoulder, saw the black lump bouncing, twisting, catching on stones, spiny plants. He dragged the man in a wide circle. Higgins no longer screamed as the rope dug into his chest, shutting off his air.

The circle completed, Morgan rode back down the alley to José's house back of El Tecolote.

He pulled up in front of a knot of people, dismounted. Captain Joe kept the rope taut as Morgan ran back to the man.

Higgins lay facedown in the dirt.

"You're hard on a man, ain't you, Morgan?" Rushmore asked. "I've got a six-gun at your back and you better be right about this man."

Carmen, José, and several deputies crowded around the bound and fallen man.

Morgan rammed a boot under Higgins's chest, flipped him over. Carmen held a lantern high. Higgins's face was streaming with blood. His shirt and vest were torn. Blood leaked from a dozen wounds, but he was alive. His eyes opened, shuttered in the lamplight.

Morgan knelt, drew his pistol. He cocked it. Held it to Higgins's head.

"Let's hear it straight, Higgins," he said quietly. "Dave Higgins. All of it. How you murdered my boy, raped my wife."

Spittle bubbled at the corners of Higgins's mouth.

"Yeah, we did it, you bastard. We all fucked your wife. Me and Luke Trask, Parsons and Matling. Trask's the onliest one left. You want him real bad, Morgan, but you won't get him. He . . . he's got a pretty little ace in the hole."

"Talk plain," Morgan said.

"You don't have all the cards. She . . ."

The spittle at the corners of Higgins's mouth turned pink. He coughed. A freshet of blood spilled from his lips. His eyes frosted, widened.

"He's dying," Rushmore said, awestruck. "You dragged him too hard."

Morgan stood up, looked at the sheriff with cold blue eyes.

"He's dying the same way my little son Tommy died, Rushmore. If he wasn't, I'd gut him out right now."

Rushmore turned away suddenly sick to his stomach.

Carmen took Morgan's arm. "Lucinda's back," she said softly. "She came in on the noon stage. She came just to see you."

"Not now, Carmen."

"Don't wait too long," she breathed. "I think . . ."

Higgins twitched, strangled on the blood that gushed up into his throat. There was a terrible rattling sound in his throat. His breath wheezed, then stopped.

"What about Trask?" Carmen whispered, jarred back to the moment, suddenly forgetting all about Lucinda Jennings waiting back there at the hotel.

"He'll come," Morgan said. "I'll be waiting."

CHAPTER TWENTY-THREE

Marie Shannon came to the El Tecolote alone. Chad Morgan stood up when she entered the front door. The place was empty, except for José behind the bar.

Morgan watched her walk slowly toward him. She wore a flowing cape over the sleek green dress. Her blonde hair tumbled over her shoulders from under the bonnet. Her shiny boots scuffed the dirt and sawdust floor. She carried a small handbag in her hand. A chain hung from her neck, an object pulling on it, hidden from view in the cleavage of her breasts.

"I'm here," she said. "You wanted to see me?"

"Yes. It took me a while to figure it out, Marie. Something I saw in your office. In the ashtray."

"The matches."

Morgan nodded. When she first walked in, he hadn't been quite sure. But Marie was too poised and now she had admitted what he had suspected. Trask had been there, in her office. He had been there for some time. The chewed-up matchsticks. Chad had seen matches just like them in Bonnie's room—their room. They'd been scattered over the floor . . . in the bedsheets. At the time, they hadn't registered. It was only when he saw some just like them in the ashtray that they had tugged at something in his mind. It had taken him a while, but he had finally remembered a habit of Trask's. One he had had back in Ellsworth . . .

The man always chewed nervously on unstruck matches.

"Why?" Morgan asked.

Marie sighed, stood there a few paces from Morgan.

"I've known Luke Trask as long as I have you. He's a man. You scorned me in Ellsworth. I hated Bonnie. I've hated her all these years."

"But Bonnie never hated anyone. She never did anyone any harm."

"She took you away from me," Marie said bitterly.

"You were never in the running, Myrtle," he said, using her given name.

Marie winced. "You've changed, Chad," she said. "There's a hardness, a coldness that wasn't there before."

"True. I can thank Trask for that. I never killed from hatred before. I never hated like I do now."

José coughed to remind them of his presence.

"Go on back in the house, José," Morgan said. "We won't be needing you. The lady's not staying. Are you, Myrtle?"

José stumped from behind the bar, left by the door that led to the kitchen.

"No," she said. "I'm not staying. I know why you wanted me here. You want Luke Trask. I can take you to him."

There was something in her voice that warned him.

She was too eager, too willing. He stepped quickly up to her, reached for the chain around her neck. He lifted the object from between her breasts.

Bonnie's wedding ring dangled on the chain.

Morgan's face turned to granite.

He gave a mighty jerk, pulling the chain from Marie's neck.

She cried out. Her hand flew to the back of the neck where the chain had broken. "Why did you do that?" she whined.

"Don't you know, Marie? Didn't Trask tell you? This ring was Bonnie's. My wife's. The woman he raped and murdered."

Marie's eyes went wide. A sob caught in her throat.

"I . . . I didn't know it was hers, Chad. You've got to believe me. It . . . it happened so fast. I . . . I thought you had . . . I believed the stories. I thought you had murdered your wife. Everybody did. Before I could stop myself, I fell in love with Trask. He came out of my past, like you. Only he came first."

Morgan saw it all now. It was sad. She had believed Luke Trask. Had fallen in love with him. Now it was too late. She had made the wrong choice. Again.

"Where's Trask?" he asked, shoving the ring and broken chain in his pants pocket.

Marie's body shook with sobs. She drew herself up, opened her purse. Morgan watched her warily. She pulled out a handkerchief, dabbed at her eyes.

"He . . . he's at the Golden Bull. I'll take you to him."

"Why? I'm going to kill him, Marie. And another man."

"Haven't you done enough killing?"

213

"Not yet."

She turned away from him, started toward the door.

Morgan walked to the bar, blew out the lamp. He went to each lamp in the room, blew them out one by one. The room sank into a hazy darkness as Marie waited by the door.

He knew Marie was lying. The odds were not good, but he needed every break he could get.

"I can't see you," she said.

"I'm here. You walk outside first. I'll stay close."

"You don't trust me, Chad."

"No."

"Who's the other man?"

"What?"

"The other man you're going to kill."

"Curly Garth."

Morgan was close to her. He felt her stiffen and pulled two wads of cotton from his shirt pocket, stuffed them in his ears, then nudged her out the door. His right hand hovered near his pistol.

He felt like he was in the shadow of the gun. He just didn't know whose gun.

The street was pitch dark. A block away, lamps burned in cantina windows. Farther down, there was more light. Shadows bulked large between the deserted buildings. The moon and stars were blotted out by heavy clouds. Another promise of rain that might not come. When he had first come to Tombstone, the clouds had been the same. The air heavy with moisture. But the weather, like man himself, was unpredictable.

A buggy and horse stood at the hitchrail.

Marie started toward it. Morgan stuck close to her. His gaze darted everywhere. It was quiet.

Too quiet.

Before she reached the buggy, Marie stopped. Morgan heard a soft thudding sound.

"I . . . I dropped my purse," she said, bending over.

Morgan knew he was exposed now.

"Have you got a match? I can't see it."

So that was how it was going to be. He was ready. Let them come.

He fingered a match from his vest pocket. He struck it on his tight trousers just under his buttocks.

The match flared into flame.

Morgan tossed the match into the air, shoved Marie facedown in the dirt. He threw himself headlong atop her.

The night exploded.

A bullet whistled over Morgan's head.

He marked the spot where the orange flame burned a hole in the fabric of night.

His pistol bucked in his hand. Once. Twice.

A cry came from between the two buildings across the street.

A man staggered into view. It was too dark to see his face.

A pistol dangled from one hand. The other hand clutched his belly.

Morgan watched him pitch forward. His hat brim struck the ground. The hat rolled away.

Curly's bald head looked like a tombstone in the darkness.

Marie moved beneath him.

"Did . . . did you kill him?" she rasped.

"That was Curly. Where's Trask hiding?"

"I don't know. I told you he's back—"

"Myrtle, don't lie to me anymore. Higgins said something before he died. He said Trask had a pretty little ace in the hole. I figure you're that ace he was talking about."

"No!"

Morgan got up, jerked her to her feet. His pistol was still in his hand, cocked.

A sound startled Morgan.

Trask wasn't where he'd expected him to be. It was worse than he thought.

The shot came quick. Deafening. Orange flame blinded him. Powder stung his face.

Luke Trask rose up in the buggy, fired straight down at Morgan. Marie twitched, grunted.

"You sonofabitch!" Trask shouted, hammering back for a second shot.

Morgan shoved Marie straight at the buggy, lifted his gun hand. He squeezed the trigger.

The bullet rammed into Trask's groin.

Trask's second shot went off. The bullet fried the air past Morgan's cottoned ear. Trask pitched forward off the buggy. Marie threw out her arms, took his weight. They both went down.

"José!" Morgan shouted back at the cantina. "Bring the lantern!"

Trask cursed, lifted his gun again.

Morgan shot him between the eyes.

Trask's legs kicked out. He fell back, mouth open in surprise, eyes frozen in a fixed stare. A stare that stretched to eternity.

Marie moved, crawling over Trask's dead body.

A lantern bobbled toward Morgan. He turned, saw José stumping along as fast as he could. Where was

Carmen? He had not seen her in an hour, had thought she was back in the house. But José was alone.

Behind him, Morgan heard an ominous click.

He whirled, hammering back instinctively.

José stopped short. The lantern threw a wedge of light over Trask's legs. Marie Shannon squatted next to Trask, holding the dead man's pistol. It was aimed straight at Morgan's chest.

The pistol wavered in her shaking hands.

"Damn you, Chad!" she hissed. "You always did mess up everything. You ruined my life back in Ellsworth. You've ruined it here."

Her breath came hard.

José stepped closer, cautiously.

The lamplight glistened on fresh blood.

"Myrtle," Morgan said softly, "you just picked the wrong man. Back in Ellsworth, here in Tombstone. I'm damned sorry for you."

A dark stain spread from just below her rib cage, over her diaphragm. She had caught Trask's first bullet. A bullet meant for him.

Marie's finger coiled around the trigger of Trask's pistol.

Morgan lifted his own pistol, took aim.

A shout stayed him from pulling the trigger.

"Chad! Don't shoot!"

Marie looked toward the sound of the voice. So did Morgan.

Carmen and Lucinda Jennings came running up from down the dark street. Both were out of breath.

"Don't kill her!" Lucinda screamed, her voice quavering with hysteria.

She threw herself at Morgan.

Marie fired point-blank.

But Lucinda's momentum shoved Chad out of the bullet's path. The lead ball whined past, thunked into soft wood.

Morgan recovered, stalked over to Marie. He reached down, snatched the pistol from her hand.

She looked up at him, mouth open, lips wet.

"You're dying, Myrtle. Marie. Whatever you call yourself. I'm sorry for you."

"It . . . it doesn't hurt," she said. "I thought it would, but it doesn't. I wanted to take you with me, Chad. But you cheated me even at that, didn't you?" Her voice was querulous, not bitter.

Morgan shook his head. "No, Marie. You cheated yourself. A man forks his own horse, rides his own trail. A woman, too, You did your own choosing. Take your blame and get back your dignity while there's still time."

He knelt beside her. Lucinda, Carmen, and José came close, looked at them.

Morgan leaned over, kissed Marie gently on the lips.

"Thanks," she breathed. "Thanks for that, Chad. My beautiful Chad."

A sob rose up in her throat, lodged there. Her breasts heaved as she struggled for the breath that was not there. The breath that would come no more. Morgan held her tightly. She shuddered and her eyes closed.

Lucinda touched Morgan on one side, Carmen on the other. He shoved his pistol back in its holster. The air smelled of burnt gunpowder, blood, and the foul odor of death.

"She . . . she loved you, Chad," Lucinda whimpered, burrowing into his side.

"I don't know," he said. "Maybe."

He turned away, putting his arms around the two girls. José let the lantern fall to his side. People began pouring into the street, walking up from where the lights winked, attracted by the sound of gunfire.

"We'll have a drink," Morgan said, "and we won't talk about this night anymore. We won't talk about the past at all."

He felt a squeeze of agreement from the two women.

Inside, he felt something digging into the flesh of his leg. He reached into his pocket, pulled out the chain and the ring.

Bonnie's ring.

"Here," he said to José, "keep this for me. I may be back for it someday."

Tears glistened in Lucinda's eyes. Carmen realized what Morgan was doing and her eyes filled as well.

"You're going away, aren't you?" Lucinda asked before they sat down. From the street came the murmur of voices.

"I reckon," Morgan said.

José took the ring, held it tight in his hand. Then he hobbled over to the bar for a bottle.

"Where will you go?" Carmen asked sadly.

"Where my horse leads me. Where memory doesn't follow like a stray cur."

"But there is no such place," Lucinda said. "You'll always be a part of Bonnie. And Tommy. They'll always be a part of you."

Glasses clinked. José poured the good whiskey, sat down with them. They drank, looking at one another over the tops of the glasses.

Morgan knew Lucinda was right. He could never

outride the memory of what he had had, but there were other things to forget, too. The killing, the bittersweet pangs of revenge. And Myrtle—Marie—the woman who had died out there on the street. A good enough woman who had struggled with her own memories. And lost.

"Listen," Carmen said.

They all heard the crackle of lightning. The windows flashed silver. The boom of thunder followed instantly. Morgan took the cotton wads from his ears.

The rains came, spanking against the windows, drumming in the street. It was a clean, good rain, a washing-away rain.

Morgan was glad that it had finally come. He drew a deep breath of the moist fresh air.

He smiled at the two women and at José.

They smiled back at him and he knew he was going to be all right. The future was there and it could never be as bad as the past. And this moment was all that there was, after all. He was living in it, and the rains had come.

"To the future," he said, raising his glass. "And to the present."

Rain rattled on the tin roof, rattled above the laughter, muffled the tears.

POWELL'S ARMY
BY TERENCE DUNCAN

#1: UNCHAINED LIGHTNING   (1994, $2.50)
Thundering out of the past, a trio of deadly enforcers dispenses its own brand of frontier justice throughout the untamed American West! Two men and one woman, they are the U.S. Army's most lethal secret weapon—they are POWELL'S ARMY!

#2: APACHE RAIDERS   (2073, $2.50)
The disappearance of seventeen Apache maidens brings tribal unrest to the violent breaking point. To prevent an explosion of bloodshed, Powell's Army races through a nightmare world south of the border—and into the deadly clutches of a vicious band of Mexican flesh merchants!

#3: MUSTANG WARRIORS   (2171, $2.50)
Someone is selling cavalry guns and horses to the Comanche—and that spells trouble for the bluecoats' campaign against Chief Quanah Parker's bloodthirsty Kwahadi warriors. But Powell's Army are no strangers to trouble. When the showdown comes, they'll be ready—and someone is going to die!

#4: ROBBERS ROOST   (2285, $2.50)
After hijacking an army payroll wagon and killing the troopers riding guard, Three-Fingered Jack and his gang high-tail it into Virginia City to spend their ill-gotten gains. But Powell's Army plans to apprehend the murderous hardcases before the local vigilantes do—to make sure that Jack and his slimy band stretch hemp the legal way!

ZEBRA'S GOT THE FINEST
IN BONE-CHILLING TERROR!

THE SURVIVALIST SERIES
by Jerry Ahern